JAN OF THE JUNGLE

Otis Adelbert Kline

Alias the Night Wind

BY VARICK VANARDY

The Blue Fire Pearl: The Complete Adventures
of Singapore Sammy, Volume 1

BY GEORGE F. WORTS

Clovelly

BY MAX BRAND

Drink We Deep

BY ARTHUR LEO ZAGAT

The Gun-Brand

BY JAMES B. HENDRYX

Minions of the Moon

BY WILLIAM GREY BEYER

The Moon Pool & The Conquest of the Moon Pool

BY ABRAHAM MERRITT

Tarzan and the Jewels of Opar

BY EDGAR RICE BURROUGHS

War Lord of Many Swordsmen:
The Adventures of Norcross, Volume 1

BY W. WIRT

JAN OF
THE JUNGLE

OTIS ADELBERT KLINE

ILLUSTRATIONS BY

JOHN R. NEILL

COVER BY

ROBERT A. GRAEF

ALTUS PRESS
2017

EDITED AND DESIGNED BY
Matthew Moring

PUBLISHING HISTORY
"Jan of the Jungle" originally appeared in the April 18 and 25, and May 2, 9, 16 and
    23, 1931 issues of *Argosy* magazine (Vol. 220, No. 3–Vol. 221, No. 2). Copyright
    © 1931 by The Frank A. Munsey Company. Copyright renewed © 1958 and
    assigned to Steeger Properties, LLC. All rights reserved.
"About the Author" originally appeared in the January 1930 issue of *The Writer*
    magazine.

ISBN
978-1-61827-304-8

Visit *altuspress.com* for more books like this.
Printed in the United States of America.

TABLE OF CONTENTS

CHAPTER I

A DIABOLICAL SCHEME

DR. BRACKEN SUAVELY bowed his Florida cracker patient out of his dispensary. It was in the smaller right wing of his rambling ancestral home on a hummock in the Everglades, near the Gulf of Mexico and five miles from Citrus Crossing.

The doctor cursed under his breath as a sudden uproar came from the larger right wing of the house, directly behind him. This wing, a place double-locked and forbidden even to his two old colored servants, had no entrance save through a narrow passageway that connected it with his private office in the smaller wing.

So far as his servants, Aunt Jenny and Uncle Henry, were concerned, a lock was superfluous. The muffled animal-like sounds that came from it were so strange and unearthly that they regarded them with superstitious awe.

As he closed the door behind his patient it seemed that a mask suddenly slipped from the doctor's face, so swift and horrible was the change that came over his features. He had been smiling and suave, but as be turned away from the door his demeanor was more like that of a frenzied madman. His teeth, bared like those of a jungle beast at bay, gleamed white and menacing against the iron-gray of his closely cropped vandyke. His small, deep-set eyes burned malevolently, madly.

Fishing a bunch of keys from his pocket, he opened the door to the narrow passageway, pressed a switch that flooded it with light, and entered, locking it behind him. The roars were louder now. At the end of the passageway he used another key to open a second door, and stepped into the room beyond, pressing a second switch as he did so. The yellow rays of a bulb overhead revealed the stoutly: barred cages that housed his private menagerie within soundproofed walls.

In the cage at his elbow an African leopard snarled menacingly. Its next-door neighbor, a South American jaguar, padded silently back and forth with head hanging low and slavering jowls slightly parted. In the adjacent cage, the bars of which had been reinforced with powerful wire meshwork, a huge python was coiled complacently around a whitewashed tree trunk, its shimmering folds resting on the shortened stumps of the limbs. Beside this was the cage of Malik, the old and nearly toothless lion.

The glittering eyes of the doctor swept the room, seeking the cause of the disturbance. They paused for a moment at the cage of Tichuk, the surly old male chimpanzee, who was squatting on his shelf, striving to look innocent. But the Brazilian spider monkeys in the cage at Tichuk's left were leaping and skipping about and chattering excitedly in a manner that showed all too plainly where the trouble had centered.

In two cages which adjoined each other and that of Tichuk were two creatures: Chicma, an old female chimpanzee, and a naked boy sixteen years of age. He was a handsome, superbly muscled lad, with a straight, athletic figure, broad shoulders, narrow hips, and the features of a Greek god, crowned by a tumbled mass of auburn curls. Several bloody scratches stood out against the white of his face and arms, and one hand still clutched a tuft of chimpanzee hair which he made no effort to conceal.

"Fighting through the bars with Tichuk again," muttered the doctor. He reached for a whip hanging on a near-by peg. Then withdrew his hand. "Won't punish him this time," he growled to himself. "Tomorrow he must perform the act of vengeance for which I have trained him. Then he will leave this

The alligator thrashed around wildly.

place forever. And I will be compensated for my years of bitterness and suffering."

Glancing at his watch, the doctor saw that it was nearly feeding time. He went into the cooler and emerged a moment later. Growls, snarls, chatterings, and rending sounds marked his, progress.

At last Chicma, the female chimpanzee, was given bet ration of bread and lettuce; but to the omnivorous manchild's ration a pound of raw beef was added.

THIS BOY, the innocent victim of the doctor's insane hatred for a woman, had never seen a human being other than the physician. Nor had he glimpsed any more of the outside world than might be observed through the small, high windows of the menagerie, or above the tall stockade just outside it, where he was exercised.

Dr. Bracken had loved the boy's mother, Georgia Adams, a titian-haired Southern beauty, with a fiery passion of which few men are capable. A sudden declaration before his departure on a trip to Africa had won what he thought was a promise from her—a half-hearted assent she had evidently regretted the moment he had gone; but it was the one thing on which he had counted during all his weary months of tramping in the jungles. Her face had smiled at him in the light of many a camp fire; her voice had soothed his troubled sleep as he lay in his net-covered hammock while fierce beasts of prey roamed just outside the *boma*. For him the red-gold sunsets had reflected the glory of her titian hair. Bits of the blue vault of heaven visible at times through rents in the forest canopy, had hinted of the more wondrous blue of her eyes.

But he had returned to America only to have the cup of happiness dashed rudely from his lips—for she had married Harry Trevor.

True, she had told him, when they had a few moments alone, of writing a letter breaking the engagement only a week after his departure. He had accepted the statement politely, yet deep in his heart he doubted it. She had broken faith, and in his estimation a woman capable of that was capable of anything. The letter, if indeed there had been a letter, had never reached him.

So love had turned to hate—an abnormally intense hate that filled his waking hours and made his nights restless and hid-eous—a passionate, unreasoning hate that engendered a desire which soon became a fixed purpose and the sole end toward which he planned and strove—revenge.

But Dr. Bracken's warped mind had cunningly pretended friendship, so cunningly that he served the Trevors as their family physician in Florida. And the birth of a son and heir gave him his long-awaited opportunity for a revenge which would be no trifling retribution from which Georgia Trevor would soon recover.

The kidnaping of the day-old boy had been ridiculously easy. At first the doctor's diabolical plan had been to mutilate and cripple the child, turn his face into a hideous monstrosity, and return him, to be a living curse to his parents. But an event had occurred in the menagerie which changed his plans and gave him the germ of an even more diabolical scheme.

For the male chimpanzee, Tichuk, at that time caged with his mate Chicma, had slain their little one in a fit of fury and was attacking her, when the doctor returned with the stolen baby. Dr. Bracken had quieted both chimpanzees with hypodermics and removed the unconscious Tichuk to another cage. Then, a terrible smile upon his face; he had skinned the baby chimpanzee, treated its hide with an odorless preservative and sewed the cotton-padded skin about the human baby. As Chicma came out of her drugged sleep he placed the child in her arms.

The chimpanzee, dazed and foggy of perception, had sniffed the hairy hide of her own child. She recognized the scent and feel; yet the tensely waiting doctor, club and whip in hand, saw her hesitate in puzzlement, as if on the verge of flinging away this somehow suspiciously changed child of hers. But nature and mother-instinct conquered, and she fed the hungry infant.

Filled with a fierce exultation, the doctor stole away, muttering:

"What a scheme! The body of a man and the mind of an ape. And I would have made a physical monster of him, but with a clear mind. She would not have recognized him—might not have acknowledged him; but now, with features unchanged, she can't deny him—and when she has seen she will die—die by the hand of her own son. I will teach him to slay. Only two words of the human language, other than his name and the names of these beasts, shall he know: 'Mother,' and 'Kill!'"

NOW, AS the demented physician looked at the sixteen-year-old ape-boy, a grin of triumph overspread his satanic features, for the awful climax of his revenge was nearly at hand.

The titian-haired woman who was the object of his hatred had come very near to dying, and thus cheating him of his full measure of vengeance, shortly after she learned that her child had been stolen. But Dr. Bracken had stood between her and death, fending off the scythe of the Grim Reaper.

For fourteen years Georgia Trevor had been an invalid—

constantly under his care. Dr. Bracken had never let her lose hope of the child's return. Then her husband, who had, meanwhile inherited the enormous fortune of his father, had purchased a palatial yacht and taken her on a two-year cruise.

Only the day before Georgia Trevor and her husband had returned to Citrus Crossing; and the doctor had planned a clever coup; a faked telegram to get the husband away from the louse, that he might consummate the revenge for which he had waited so long, and for which he had trained the boy from babyhood.

Dr. Bracken, who had a liking for things oriental, had named the boy "Jan," after Jan ibn Jan who, in Arabic legends, was Sultan of the Evil Jinn. A truly demoniac name—the choice of a diabolical mind.

As the raw meat was thrown to him, Jan who was a perfect mimic, seized it with a snarl as he had seen the carnivora seize theirs. While the doctor watched, seated in his chair, with a long black stogie going, the lad retired, growling, to a corner of his cage. First he ate the meat; then he munched a few lettuce leaves. The rest of his rations he passed through the bars to his foster-mother.

When Jan had finished his meal, the doctor arose, took his whip from the peg, and opened the doors of their cages. Then he shouted: "Jan! Chicma!" and whistled as if he were calling a dog. The boy and chimpanzee came out.

The doctor walked to a door which had been cut in the end of the menagerie wing a number of years before, and opened it. While he fumbled with the latch, the imitative lad, unobserved, opened the catch of the lion's cage, leaving the door slightly ajar. Then he and the chimpanzee obediently followed the doctor out of the building into a stockade with a twelve-foot board fence around it. In this stockade were various exercising devices—a trapeze, parallel bars, a thick rope for climbing, and a suspended dummy dressed like a woman, with titian hair.

For some time the boy and ape amused themselves by swing-

ing on the trapeze and rope. Then they performed various antics
on the parallel bars.

Presently the doctor called them down from the bars.
Walking to the dummy of the red-haired woman, he shook it
savagely and said:

"Mother! Kill!"

Instantly the boy and ape charged the dummy, biting and
tearing with mimic ferocity, the ape snarling and growling, but
the boy, between his own snarls and growls, crying: "Mother!
Kill!"

Both boy and ape always enjoyed this mimic fight which
ended their afternoon exercises, and were loath to leave off
when the doctor whistled to them.

But before he could summon them a second time there came
a terrific growl from the doorway behind them. Turning, he
beheld Malik, the old lion, just emerging from the door. With
upraised whip he tried to frighten the beast into returning to
its cage, but it snarled and raised a huge paw menacingly.

He flicked the lion on the nose, and it backed up with a
growl. Again he stung the tender nose, and the lion slunk,
snarling, back into the house. Here it was necessary once more
to use the lash in order to get the stubborn feline to enter the
cage. When the beast was inside, the doctor shut and fastened
the door, and with a sigh of relief took his handkerchief from
his pocket and mopped his dripping face.

But his look of relief was instantly supplanted by one of fierce
anger as he realized that it must have been Jan who opened the
catch of that cage door. Well, Jan must be taught a lesson. He
should receive a whipping that he would not soon forget.

Gripping his whip more tightly and frowning thunderously, the doctor strode menacingly through the door. But after
one look around the stockade he gasped in astonishment.

Jan and Chicma were gone!

AT THE first growl of the lion from the doorway, Chicma,
who had an intense hereditary fear of the king of beasts, ran,

and seizing the end of the climbing rope swung high in the air. At the end of her swing she was only a few feet from the top of the fence which surrounded the stockade. Letting go of the rope, and still carried onward by the momentum of her swing, she caught the top of the fence with both forepaws, drew herself up, and dropped to the ground on the other side.

Jan was not nearly so frightened by the growl of the lion. But he was at the imitative age, and the beast that had just gone over the fence was, so far as his knowledge went, his parent. Fully as agile as the chimpanzee and nearly as strong, it was easy for him to swing up onto the fence and follow.

Still thoroughly frightened, she was standing fifty feet away from the fence in a patch of saw-palmettos, bouncing up and down and calling to him in the language of the chimpanzees— the only language Jan fully understood:

"Come, come! Hurry, or Malik the Terrible One will eat you!"

As soon as his feet struck the ground she scampered off through the palmettos, swinging along on hind toes and fore-knuckles. Jan, who had never traveled for any great distance, followed, imitating her peculiar gait for a while, but presently found that he could keep up with her much better by traveling on only two legs, as the doctor traveled.

He was without clothing of any kind, and the saw-edged leaves cruelly lacerated his tender skin, so he was soon a mass of bloody scratches. His feet, bruised and cut by sticks and sharp stones, left spots of red on the ground. But all of these hurts only served to accelerate his speed. He imagined that the shrubs were angry with him for some unknown reason, and, like Dr. Bracken with his whip, were punishing him. He must get away from them, as Chicma was doing.

They crossed a hummock on which a few tall, gaunt, long-needle pines stood like silent sentinels. Beyond this the ground became marshy, so they were sometimes wading ankle-deep in muck, sometimes sunk to the armpits in mud water, and sub-aqueous vegetation.

This was Jan's first sight of the outside world, and despite the hurts he was getting, he was thrilled immeasurably Freedom—the only condition that makes life tolerable and desirable to men who have spirit—was his for the first time. It went to his head like strong wine. He shouted—a wordless, triumphant roar, voicing the exuberance of his feelings.

Everywhere about him were new sights smells and sounds. With the soft mud oozing up between his toes, the warm water splashing around his legs, and the hot sun beating mercilessly down on his tousled red head and bare body, he strode happily onward.

PRESENTLY THEY came to another hummock, on which grew several wild orange trees. Chicma sprang into one of these and began to regale herself with the highly acid fruit, and Jan followed her example.

The sun was low on the western horizon when they came to a forest of cypress and water oaks, most of which were standing in the water. They were heavily draped with Spanish moss and Jan, who was wont to personalize everything, compared the bearded trees with the bearded doctor, and heartily disliked them for the similarity.

Scarcely had they entered the shady depths ere Jan heard, far off in the direction whence they had come a weird sound that sent gooseflesh crawling all over his body.

Chicma heard it, too, and although she had been traveling slowly before, redoubled her speed, urging Jan in her queer chimpanzee gutturals to hurry after her. Jan had heard similar sounds before, and they had always, caused the gooseflesh to come up on his skin even though he had no idea that they were the baying of bloodhounds trailing some luckless Negro who was attempting to escape from the convict camp.

Chicma sensed that the creatures were on their trail, so she sprang into a tree, calling to Jan to follow her, just as two huge bloodhounds, their quarry in sight, plunged forward with eager barks to seize them.

For a moment Jan stood, looking curiously at the advancing creatures. Then he turned, and with a dexterous leap, caught one of the lower branches of a water oak. Swinging his lithe body up into a tree, he was climbing, and watching the dogs, now leaping and barking beneath him, when he was startled by a thunderous growl just above him.

By this time the darkness had deepened to such an extent that he could not see clearly, but as he glanced fearfully upward, he beheld a tremendous black bulk, from which two gleaming, phosphorescent eyes looked down at him.

Then a huge paw tipped with sharp, sickle-like claws, swung for his upturned face.

CHAPTER II

IN THE BEARDED FOREST

AS SOON AS he discovered that Jan and Chicma were not in the stockade, Dr. Bracken realized that they must, somehow, have got over the fence. Although he was a wiry and powerful man, the doctor was unable to leap high enough to grasp the top of the twelve foot barrier that confronted him, nor did Chicma's method occur to him.

To have Jan seen at large with one of his chimpanzees would mean the destruction, of all his plans, and perhaps of himself. Lynchings were not unknown, and the monstrous crime he had committed would arouse these people to a killing frenzy.

He dashed around the house to where the stockade jutted out from the menagerie. Here his trained hunter's eye quickly found the tracks where Jan and Chicma had alighted, and he hurried away on the trail, feeling confident of being able to soon overtake his fleeing quarry. He smiled when he saw the spots of blood mingled with the boy's footprints, for he believed that the lad would not long endure the pain of attempting to escape.

He crossed the stretch of saw palmetto and the pine-crested hummock with speed and confidence, but when he entered the marsh on the other side he lost the trail time and again where the tracks were concealed under water, and only found it by repeated circling and searching. This took time, and time, to him was very precious, for he knew that while he was floundering about, there in the muck and water, his quarry was getting farther away.

After about a half hour he decided that he would save time in the end by going back and borrowing a pair of bloodhounds from the sheriff.

He made the excuse that one of his apes had escaped; but it was with great difficulty that he dissuaded the sheriff from accompanying him on the hunt.

The hounds made much swifter progress than the doctor, so much so that they were soon out of sight, and he was able to follow them only by the sound of their baying.

He had traveled a considerable distance into the marsh when he met a Seminole Indian named Pete Little, whom he had often seen around Citrus Crossing.

"You make big hunt?" the Indian asked.

"Yes. One of my apes got away."

"I seen it," said Pete, and cast a look at the doctor that was full of meaning. "Red-head boy with it, about sixteen, seventeen year old."

"Yes?"

"Mrs. Trevor, she's red-headed. Her baby boy was stole sixteen year ago."

"And—"

"I poor. You rich. For thousand dollar I forget."

"I think that can be arranged," said the doctor, his face suddenly gone pale. His perfectly controlled features betrayed no other sign of his emotion. He added suddenly, with feigned terror: "Look there, behind you! A moccasin!"

At the sound of that dread word, the Indian turned. He saw no moccasin, but realized too late that he had been tricked. There was a sharp report, a stinging pain that shot through his left side like the searing of a hot iron—and oblivion. As he pitched forward on his face in the muck, the doctor holstered his smoking forty-five, kicked viciously at the prostrate form, and hurried on after the baying bloodhounds, whose distant cries had suddenly changed to fighting growls.

CHAPTER III

JAN'S FIRST FIGHT

AS THE SICKLE-LIKE claws of the big creature above him swung for his face, Jan dodged and hastily scuttled out on the limb. But the cornered black bear was not to be so easily dismissed. With a blood-curdling roar, it plunged down after the naked youth. At this, the blood-hounds below increased their clamor, leaping and barking with redoubled fury.

But the limb that Jan occupied, and onto which the beast had suddenly flung itself, was not equal to the combined weight of boy and brute, and gave way with a resounding crack.

Clutching wildly in mid-air, Jan grasped the tip of a branch which projected from an adjoining tree. It sagged with his weight, but did not break, and with his ape-like agility it was not difficult for him to quickly scramble to a less precarious position beside the trunk.

The bear; meanwhile, crashed to the ground, where it was instantly set upon by the dogs. A thud, and a series of plaintive yelps from one of them indicated that the creature, despite its fall was able to give a good account of itself. A medley of fierce barking, snarling and growling followed. But the bear, harassed by the dogs but not particularly fearful of them, lumbered away through the dark forest, crashing through the underbrush and splashing through the pools. Presently the sounds of its movements died away, and there drifted to Jan only the barking of the hounds, which were evidently still worrying their quarry.

Then it was that a new sound came to the alert ears of the

young fugitive—the sound of a man, crashing and splashing among the trees. Looking in the direction of the sound, Jan saw a bright light moving through the forest.

As he was watching the approach of the man with mingled curiosity and fear, Chicma suddenly swung herself into the tree beside him.

"Come," she barked, "or Cruel One will get us! Follow me!"

Jan understood that by "Cruel One," she meant Dr. Bracken. All the occupants of their small menagerie world had been similarly named to him by his foster mother. The lion was "Terrible One," the jaguar "Fierce One," the snake "Sleepy One," and the monkeys "Chattering Ones," words which would have been nothing more than guttural grunts and barks to anyone else, but each of which had a distinct meaning for Jan.

Frightened at the very mention of Dr. Bracken, Jan hurried after the chimpanzee, as she swung from tree to tree, taking a direction opposite that of the hounds and the great beast they were harrying.

Presently, as they moved away among the cool, leafy branches, the sounds made by the doctor died away, and his flashlight was no longer visible. A little later, Jan could not hear the hounds, and the only noises that came to his ears were the natural sounds of the swamp—the hoarse booming of frogs, the chirping of crickets, the humming of insects, and the cries of night birds.

Tired and hungry, Jan besought his foster mother to stop, but she would not do so until the very edge of the forest was reached, and they could no longer proceed without descending to the ground. She then curled up in the crotch of a tree, and the weary youth was glad to follow her example.

JAN WAS awakened by a call from Chicma. Hot sunlight was streaming down on his face through a rift in the branches. Looking down, he beheld the chimpanzee devouring some berries she was gathering from some low bushes that grew along the bank of a tiny stream which meandered through the marsh.

He leaned over to call to her, and as he did so, felt numerous twinges on his back, neck and arms, which changed his cry to one of pain. His limbs and body were bright red in color and felt extremely hot, while touching them caused a burning sensation that was anything but pleasant. There were many small red bumps, too, which itched intolerably, and these combined with the scratches he had received made the boy more uncomfortable than he had ever felt before. It was Jan's first experience with sunburn and mosquito bites in such heroic doses.

Hearing his cry of pain, Chicma looked up and called softly to him. At this instant the head of an alligator emerged from the water behind her, and the powerful jaws seized her by the arm. She screamed wildly in anguish. As she was being dragged into the water she gripped the thick roots of a cypress with her other arm and hung on, while the reptile shook and tugged, in an effort to break her hold and drag her into the stream.

Jan, who had been about to make a gingerly descent on account of his many hurts, on seeing this attack on his foster-parent, ignored his own soreness and dropped swiftly from limb to limb until he stood beside her. Then, with a snarl like that of a wild beast, he leaped astride the saurian's back, and bit, scratched and pummeled the armored enemy with no apparent effect except the damage to his own fists. He sought for a hold on the creature's head, to pull it away from Chicma, and his hands came in contact with two round bumps on top of the head. In these bumps were soft spots. Plunging the middle finger of each hand into one of these, he pulled backward.

At this, the alligator instantly let go its hold on its victim, and backed, wildly threshing, into the water. For Jan had found its eyes—the two most vulnerable points on its entire anatomy. Blinded, and with every bit of fight taken out of it, the reptile thrashed about in the shallow water, its sole object to escape those gouging fingers and unseat the creature on its back. As a result, Jan was thrown into the water, whence he floundered quickly to the shore, while the alligator, bent only on escape, glided to the center of the stream where it sank out of sight.

When Jan reached the bank, Chicma had climbed up into the tree and was whimpering and licking her wounded arm. He called to her to come down—that the danger from the monster had passed—but she was so badly frightened that she paid no heed to him.

This was Jan's first battle with anything other than the red-headed dummy of a woman which Cruel One had provided. He had, of course, played at fighting with Chicma many times, for she had, to the best of her ability, instructed him in the arts of defense and offense, but this was his first real fight, and he had won. He had conquered a very terrible monster of which even Chicma was afraid.

His chest swelled with pride as he strode stiffly up and down the muddy bank, calling the alligator all manner of disagreeable chimpanzee names, and inviting it to come back for more punishment. He tired of this presently, when the reptile did not reappear, and set to work to still the craving of his empty stomach by plucking and eating the berries which grew in profusion thereabout. He quickly learned to distinguish between green and ripe berries.

JAN'S VICTORY over the alligator made him feel superior to the ape—and whereas he had previously believed her greater than himself, both mentally and physically, he now knew, instinctively, that this was not the case. His man mind had begun to assert itself—to take its natural place in the scale of creation. He was stronger and braver than Chicma, and a greater fighter. She might betray her weakness and inferiority by whimpering, but as for him, no matter how great the pain, he would henceforth suffer in silence.

They traveled without food until late in the afternoon, when they came to the lonely cabin of one of the dwellers in the swamp. After reconnoitering to make sure that there was no one about they raided a garden which yielded sweet potatoes, celery, lettuce and tomatoes, with some luscious grapefruit off a nearby tree for dessert.

When they had eaten their fill, they resumed their journey, traveling toward the reddening disk of the setting sun. But they had not gone far when there came to the ears of Jan a strange and fearful sound. It seemed to him an incongruous combination of whispering and roaring, and his active young imagination immediately set to work to picture the monster that could make so voluminous and terrible a sound.

He hesitated, fearful of venturing farther in the direction of the noise but as Chicma advanced unperturbed, and as he now felt himself braver and greater than she, he marched on beside her with no outward sign of the trepidation he felt.

It was not long before they came to what was to Jan a most amazing sight. It was a broad, curved beach of gleaming white sand with white-crested waves rolling in, dashing a fine spray high in the air and leaving a line of silvery spume at the point where they receded.

Chicma walked out upon the smooth white sand, and turned to the left. Jan, perturbed but resolute, walked beside her. The sand felt soft and pleasant to his injured feet, and it was not long before he gathered sufficient courage to walk out into the spume. This felt exceptionally pleasant until the salt began to smart his wounds, whereupon he imagined that the sea was becoming angry with him, and quickly retreated to the dry sands.

The sun was just disappearing into the evening mists with a last blaze of blood-red glory when they arrived at the bank of a small rivulet that flowed into the Gulf. A few coconut trees adorned its banks, and Chicma instantly climbed one of these, throwing a half dozen large nuts to the ground. She then descended and Jan, always quick to mimic followed her example as she tore the fibrous covering with her sharp teeth.

When she had uncovered the end of the inner shell she broke this open with a stone and eagerly drank the liquid it contained.

Jan also picked up a stone and bashed in the end of his coconut. He tasted the milk gingerly at first, then drained it with great relish. He was discovering more good things all the time in this strange outer world which had been withheld from him for so long.

But there was more to come, for Chicma, removing more of the fibrous outer wrapping, proceeded to break off pieces of the inner shell and devour the white, tasty nut meat that adhered to it. Jan did likewise, and found another delight.

But Chicma did not open a second nut, for there suddenly sounded above the roar of the surf, an ominous rumble accompanied by a white flash, far out over the Gulf. Calling Jan to follow her, the chimpanzee hurried into the thickest part of the underbrush in the coconut grove, and there crouched, shivering with her fear of the lightning.

Jan could not understand this fear. Unperturbed, he looked out over the Gulf in the direction of the noise. The rumblings were becoming louder, and the flashes brighter. The last red glow of sunset was being swallowed up by a tumbling mass of blue-black clouds. But these things were, to him, rather commonplace, for he had often seen approaching thunder clouds through the high windows of the menagerie, and several times had viewed them from the stockade.

What principally attracted his attention was a most puzzling thing on the surface of the water. It appeared to have a pair of large, white wings, placed one in front of the other, which did not flap like those of birds, but were held more or less rigidly, straight up in the air. He was astonished to see one of the wings swiftly disappear, followed in a moment by the disappearance of the other. On the back of the thing were tiny moving creatures that looked, at a distance, to be much like Cruel One.

Jan did, not know that what he had seen was not an animal, but a Venezuelan schooner, which had scurried to anchor behind a sheltering point of land and then lowered sail, in order to escape the fury of the coming storm. Nor had he any means of knowing that one of the figures on the deck had been scanning the shore with binoculars and had seen both Jan and Chicma— a naked boy and an African ape—here on the western coast of Florida.

A short time after Jan crouched down beside the cowering Chicma, the storm broke.

CAPTAIN FRANCESCO Santos, commander and owner of the schooner *Santa Margarita,* brushed back the straggling hairs of his small, coal-black mustache, inserted a cigarette between his coarse lips, and lit it.

Filling his lungs with tobacco smoke, he exhaled slowly and as he did so, addressed Jake Grubb, his powerful, blond bearded first mate, who was peering at the shore through a pair of binoculars.

"*Por Dios,* Señor Grubb! You seem to 'ave locate' sometheeng that ees of more interest than the coming storm. May I 'ave the look, also?"

"I seen it, but I don't believe it," replied Grubb, handing his binoculars to Santos.

Santos turned the glass in the direction indicated, and focused it to suit his vision.

"Son of wan gun, *señor!*" he exclaimed. "It ees not the *bacardi,* for I see them also, and me, I drank *tequila.*"

"What are they a doin' now, captain?"

"The ape ees just take what you call the duck into the bushes. The boy ees stand there and look at us. The ape ees scared, but that boy, he's not afraid of notheeng, I tal you."

A particularly loud clap, of thunder, followed by the spatter of raindrops and a violent tilting of the schooner as the storm broke, sent both men scurrying for cover. Once inside the cabin, Santos lit another cigarette and got out his bottle of *tequila,* while Grubb resorted to his pipe and his rum.

"What would you think, captain, if I told you I had an idea for makin' some easy money?" asked Grubb, refilling his glass and sucking at his pipe.

"I would be delight', *señor,* if I, Francesco Santos, could thereby make what you call the honest penny."

"I believe," said Grubb, "in takin' what the good Lord provides. Over there, hidin' in the bushes, is some kind of a big African ape. It may be a gorilla or it may be a chimpanzee, but I know from its looks that it's one or the other. It must have got away from some circus, because apes like that don't run wild anywhere except in Africa. People were payin' good money to see that critter, and they'll do it again. I traveled with a street carnival for one season, and barked on a side-show door with a circus, so I know something about the racket. If we catch that ape, bring it aboard, and build a cage for it, we kin turn this schooner into a showboat. Or we kin buy a tent, travel from port to port in ease and style, and stay in each place as long as the dough rolls in. There ain't no limit to where we kin go, what we kin do, or how much we kin make."

"*Carramba!* That sound pretty good, *amigo.* One hour before daylight, then, we leave for the shore weeth nets and ropes. I dreenk to our success *amigo.*"

"Down the hatch," replied Grubb, as he tossed off his drink.

CHAPTER IV

CAPTURED

JAN WAS AWAKENED by a low cry of warning from Chicma. Then he heard the sound of human voices. The darkness had passed, and a pink glow heralded the coming of the sun.

The voices grew louder—closer, and there were crashing sounds in the underbrush all around them. As these drew nearer, Chicma, calling softly to the boy to follow, made a sudden rush to break through the narrowing circle.

As she leaped out of the bushes, the ape tried to dart between two men who stood about ten feet apart. One was a swarthy fellow with a small mustache. The other was jet black, and gigantic in stature. But as she ran forward, the two suddenly lifted a net which they had been trailing between them, and in a moment she was struggling in its meshes which the two men drew tighter and tighter around her.

Bewildered by the strange sights and sounds, Jan dashed off into the undergrowth, but when he saw that Chicma had been caught he paused, hoping to see her break away. As it became increasingly evident to him that she would not be able to do this unaided, he snarled like an enraged animal—then charged.

The two men were bending over Chicma as she thrashed on the ground, attempting to put ropes on her. Four others, three with brown skins and one with a bushy yellow beard, were running toward them carrying nets and ropes. Paying no heed to these reinforcements, Jan leaped on the back of the man nearest him—the swarthy fellow with the little mustache—and growling and snarling like a jungle beast, attacked him with teeth and nails.

But the yellow-bearded giant ran up behind him and pulled him off.

Quick as a flash, Jan turned on this new enemy and sank his teeth into the hairy forearm. With an exclamation of pain and anger, the big man jabbed a huge fist into the boy's midriff, causing him to let go his hold and gasp for breath. The fist flashed out a second time, colliding with his jaw, and Jan's whirling senses left him.

Jan did not know when he was bundled aboard the ship, nor could he know that his jailer of sixteen years, Dr. Bracken, had resumed his trailing, after daybreak, just a bit too late. The signs of struggle and capture were plain enough, and Bracken furiously followed the tracks down to the shore, where the marks of a boat's prow were etched deep in the sand. Looking out across the bay he saw a small schooner flying the flag of Venezuela. He could not make out her name. Even as he looked, her sails were raised and her anchor hoisted. Then slowly, gracefully, the vessel sailed around the point and southward. The half-maddened doctor knew that for the time being, at least, his vengeful pursuit was balked.

WHEN JAN recovered consciousness once more, he was in a strange half-dark place of queer sights, sounds, smells and motions. There was a thick collar around his neck, fastened by a heavy chain to a large ring in the planking behind him. A little way from him; and trying to reach him, but held by her chain in a similar manner to a ring on the opposite side of the space they occupied, was Chicma.

She called softly to him, and when he answered, seemed satisfied by the assurance that he was alive, and quit tugging at her chain.

Through the cracks between the boards on, which he lay, and which constantly lurched under him with a motion that gave

Jan a most unpleasant feeling, he could hear the swishing of bilge water, which stank abominably. Some mildewed excelsior had been scattered over the planking, and the sour odor of this only increased the wave of nausea that swept over him.

For hours that seemed interminable, he lay there, constantly swayed by the lurching of the ship, and suffering in silence.

Then a hatch was raised there was the sound of voices and footsteps descending the ladder, and the swarthy man with the little mustache, came through the door. Just behind him was the huge individual with the yellow beard.

Jan instinctively hated all men with beards because Dr. Bracken was bearded. And to top this instinctive dislike was the fact that this particular bearded man had injured him.

The two men were talking. But Jan, of course, was unable to understand them. The fact that they were looking at him, however, was enough. He growled menacingly.

"I'll be hanged if that kid ain't wilder than the chimpanzee," said Jake Grubb. He walked closer to Jan and held out a hand placatingly. "Come here, boy. What's yer name?"

Jan bared his teeth with a fierce snarl, and snapped at the hand which was hastily withdrawn.

"Blood of the devil!" exclaimed Santos with mock-consternation. "Look out, *señor*. You will be devoured."

"You know, captain, I b'lieve this kid'll make a better drawin' card than the ape," said Grubb. "We kin show 'em in a cage together—the African wild man and the African ape. We'll have to make the boy some kind of a breech clout or skirt out of hide."

"So, *amigo*? And who weel persuade heem to wear it?"

"I'll make him wear it or break his back," replied Grubb.

CHAPTER V

THE ROPE'S END

FOR MANY HOURS, Jan lay on the floor, rising only to drink at intervals from a pan of water which the men had gingerly slid into his cage.

But the sea grew calmer, the rocking of the craft became less violent and gradually his seasickness left him. And he grew very hungry.

Although Chicma had been fed several times during this period, Jan's original ration remained untouched; and he was given nothing more to eat. A huge black man—the one who had helped to capture the chimpanzee—had come in once and refilled his water pan for him. Jan had growled at this giant as he had at the others, but the man had talked softly, soothingly, to him, and had been very deliberate in his movements, so the boy had made no attempt to molest him as he poured the water into the pan from the pitcher.

With his appetite back and his sickness gone, Jan drank the last of the water which the black giant had left for him. Then he ate the bananas set before him—a fruit of which he was very fond. But the cold chili burned him with its pepper, and he quickly spat out the first mouthful. But the smell of the meat in it urged him on. Scooping up another mouthful, he chewed it rapidly, and swallowed it. This mouthful seemed to bite him a little, but not nearly so much as the first. Quickly he finished the contents of the bowl.

His stomach filled, Jan was stretching out in his excelsior when he heard the voices of men descending the ladder.

Tensely alert, he sat up as two men entered the room. The foremost was the yellow-bearded white man he had learned to dislike so intensely. Behind him walked the giant Negro. The white man carried a short stout rope and a roll of leather. The Negro carried a pitcher, with which he refilled the pans of Chicma and Jan while the first mate unrolled his leather bundle.

"Now, Borno," said Grubb, "I'll show you how to dress up this kind. Might have to dress him down before I dress him up, but that's all in a day's work."

"*Oui, m'sieu',*" acquiesced Borno, who was a Haitian Negro, and actually though not nominally the second mate of the *Santa Margarita*. "*Oui, m'sieu',* I watch."

The leather which Grubb had unrolled was a short skirt, slightly resembling a Highlander's kilts, and attached to a stout belt. Holding this spread out in his two huge hands, he slowly advanced toward Jan, who backed away with a snarl.

"Needn't to act thataway. Ain't goin' to hurt ye none," said Grubb. But his actions belied his words, for he made a sudden spring, clasping the belt around the boy's waist, and lifting him from the floor.

Squirming, kicking, clawing, Jan was soon dangling with the belt beneath his armpits, still unbuckled. With cat-like quickness, he doubled up and bit clear through one of Grubb's hands.

Roaring a blood-curdling oath, the first mate dropped him and backed away, nursing his wounded hand. Then, flinging down the leather skirt, he caught up the rope he had brought.

JAN DID not cower as the big man advanced toward him, but strained at his chain in his endeavor to reach his enemy. Standing just out of his reach, the mate brought down the end of the rope with a skill that came of long practice, and a little stream of blood trickled downward, from the welt it made in Jan's tender, sunburned skin.

Again and again he swung the cruel rope, blood spurting

from a new welt at each blow. But not so much as the slightest
whimper escaped the lips of Jan. Instead, he strained at his
collar until it nearly choked him in his attempts to reach his
cruel foe. And in his glittering eyes was the light of a killing
frenzy.

Aroused by this mistreatment of her foster child, and by the
smell of blood, Chicma also was tugging at her chain, endeavoring to go to the boy's rescue while voicing her anger in force-
ful chimpanzee invective, and gnashing her powerful teeth until
her pendulous lips and hairy chest were flecked with saliva.

Borno watched the proceedings calmly at first, but when the
body of the boy was a mass of bloody welts and his spirit remained unbroken, his eyes glittered with a light that echoed
the look in those of Jan, and his thick lips compressed in an
expression of disapproval.

"Zis is too much for Borno," he growled at the mate, and
went up on deck.

Chicma, who had been jumping up and down, now turned,
and grasping her chain in both front paws, braced her hind feet
against the wall and pulled. Jan, who was as quick to see the
advantage of this means of leverage as he was to imitate, followed her example. He was stronger and heavier than the ape,
and the staple which held the ring pulled out, dropping him
on his bloody back on the rough planking.

More amused than perturbed by this incident, Grubb laughed
and cut at the boy's unprotected chest and abdomen with his
bloody rope.

But it was only for an instant that Jan remained on the floor.
With lightning quickness he rolled out of reach, then leaped
to his feet and faced his tormentor. Grubb instantly followed
him, and had his rope upraised for another blow when Jan
seized the heavy chain which hung from his collar and, imitating his attacker, swung it back in retaliation. It caught the first
mate a terrific blow across the face, half stunning him for an

instant. But before Jan could swing it a second time the man leaped for him.

Unhampered now by the chain, it would have been easy for the youth to dodge beneath the extended arms. But he had no thought of flight. Instead of attempting to escape, he leaped on the back of his enemy. There flashed to him, at this instant, the memory of the manner in which he had vanquished the alligator. And he did not doubt that this new enemy might be overcome in the same manner. Lightning-quick to act on any impulse, Jan found the two soft vulnerable spots and plunged in gouging fingers.

With a shriek of anguish, Grubb seized the boy and flung him over his head. But swift as his action had been, it was far too slow to save his eyes from torture.

Unhurt by his fall, Jan sprang to his feet to face a totally changed enemy. Instead of menacing him with the cruel rope, the mate was now holding his hands over his face and groaning. But such conduct only added contempt to Jan's hatred. Again he swung his heavy chain, cutting Grubb across his unprotected middle.

With a shriek of fear, the mate groped for the door, and hastily climbed the ladder. But Jan, his anger unsated, followed him, relentlessly swinging his heavy chain.

When Borno, having sickened at the sight of the cruelty practiced on Jan reached the deck, he found Captain Santos scanning the horizon with his binoculars.

"'Ave you dress the boy so soon?" Santos asked, as he struck a match on the side of the cabin.

"Non, m'sieu' le capitain," replied the Negro respectfully. "I theenk you better stop M'sieu' Grubb from use zat rope. Zat boy he's never geeve up until he dead. Borno know."

Santos laughed nastily. "You lak the young devil pretty well, heh? You don't lak to see heem hurt. Well, I tal you sometheeng. Thees Grubb knows hees beesiness. He's 'andle many men—

'undreds, thousands. He's 'andle man or boy wan time, that wan nex' time ees do what Señor Grubb tal heem."

They both whirled at a sudden sound.

"Nombre de Dios!" Santos cried. "What 'as 'appen to you, *señor?"*

But Grubb, who had just emerged from the hatchway, blood streaming down his face, neither saw nor heard them. Shrieking his fear and anguish, he ran aimlessly hither and thither across the deck. And following him grimly, relentlessly, was Jan, bloody but unconquered, swinging his heavy chain regularly and effectively.

AT EACH thud of the chain Grubb tripped over a coil of rope and shrieked and ran. Once he fell. But he was on his feet again in an instant, running as if the very devil were after him. Santos and Borno sprang forward to rescue the mate. But they were far too slow. Before they shad taken a dozen steps they saw him blunder against the rail and pitch overboard.

Both men instantly hurried to the rail, Santos hastily snatching a life preserver while he watched the water for the mate's reappearance. His head bobbed up, and the captain cast the circle of inflated rubber. But the mate could not see it.

Following the ship at a pace that matched its own, several large sail-like fins protruded from the water. The two men saw them converge toward the struggling human figure.

"Maria Madre!" exclaimed Santos. "Sharks! It ees the end!"

One fin, nearer than the others, suddenly disappeared. The bobbing head went down with a final, despairing shriek. There was a flashing and darting hither and thither of other fins and the water was churned to a pink foam.

Both men had, for the time, forgotten the presence of the red-haired youth. They found him lying unconscious beside the rail in a pool of his own blood, the heavy chain still gripped in his fingers.

Borno lifted him as tenderly as if Jan had been his own child.

"*Maîtresse Ezilée*," he prayed to his Voodoo goddess, "give zis boy hees life, hees health."

Gathering Jan to his broad black bosom, he carried him down the ladder and gently laid him on his bed of excelsior.

CHAPTER VI

HURRICANE

WEAKENED BY THE terrific loss of blood from his many wounds Jan did not recover consciousness for some time. When he did, he noticed that beneath him there was some thing softer and more pleasant to lie upon than he had ever felt in his life before. Borno, who squatted near him watching anxiously, had brought one of his own blankets to throw over the rough excelsior.

As Jan opened his eyes, Borno talked soothingly to the youth, who lay there, too sick to show either resentment or appreciation. Presently the Negro, who knew from experience the thirst that comes to the severely wounded, proffered the pan of water. Jan made a feeble effort to sit up, but his head swam and he sank back.

His huge hand gentle as that of a woman, Borno helped the youth to raise his head and held the pan to his lips. Jan drank eagerly, deeply—then looked his thanks at the big Negro and lay back once more, closing his eyes.

Borno rose and quietly left the room. Mounting the ladder, he met Santos

"Pardon, m'sieu', but I don' theenk zat boy need to be chain'," he said. "He's ver' seeck boy."

"Weeth our own eyes we saw what he did to Señor Grubb," replied the captain. "Me, I would rather see *el tigre* loose on my ship."

As Santos's native language was Spanish and Borno's Haitian

Creole, the common ground was English, which both under-stood fairly well, as did the members of the *mestizo* crew, who were from Jamaica and Trinidad.

"Zat boy ees need planty sunlight—fresh air," persisted Borne, "or he's gone die."

"Maybe you like to make the cage for heem on deck," suggested Santos. "Then we can take off the chain."

"I make ze cage, *m'sieu'*," promised Borne eagerly.

And so it came about that in a few days, during which the *Santa Margarita* had sped steadily southward, Jan and Chicma were installed in an airy, sunlit cage on the deck, where they could breathe the fresh salt breeze, uncontaminated by the scent of bilge water, mildewed excelsior, and the lingering ghosts of previous smelly cargoes which haunted the hold.

Borno insisted on not only feeding, but personally attending to the wants of the boy and ape. And both soon became so friendly toward him that he could enter the cage without fear of attack, although if Santos, the steward Audrey, or any of the others approached the bars they met with unmistakable signs of hostility.

From the start, Borno attempted to establish communication with the boy through speech, using broken English rather than his Haitian Creole, as it was the language spoken on the ship. Failing in this, he resorted to simple words and signs. It was not long before he found that Jan only knew four words: his own name, that of Chicma, and "Mother! Kill!"

The big Negro then set out to teach him to speak, and with considerable success. Despite his former lack of human association, Jan had a quick, bright mind, and once he discovered the purpose of the Negro's patient drilling, was eager to learn. Each day he added a few words to his meager vocabulary, which, when Borno was away, he took great pleasure in repeating over and over again to Chicma, much to her puzzlement.

FROM A number of tanned jaguar skins, which had been rejected by New Orleans fur buyers because of shot holes and other imperfections, Borno fashioned three garments. Understanding the imitative nature of Jan and Chicma, he entered the cage and put on one which he had made for himself. He did this several times before Jan followed his example and donned the garment which Borno had given him. Several days later Chicma also put on her jaguar skin. And within two weeks all were wearing them.

Borno tried taking his off, but this wouldn't work, for each time he did this the youth and ape promptly removed theirs. So he was forced to go about in his primitive attire, much to the secret amusement of the other members of the crew—secret, because they all feared the mighty thews of the giant Negro.

The captain said that as soon as they made port the exhibition would commence. Borno was to represent an African savage who had assisted in the capture of the chimpanzee and wild boy in their native haunts. Santos was composing a colorful and highly imaginative ballyhoo to be used as soon as he could get a tent erected in the first South American port.

But before they could make port there was an unforeseen occurrence which the carefully laid plans of the embryo showman had not included.

Borno was returning from feeding his two charges, when he encountered Santos, very much agitated. The sails were flapping idly—barely moving the ship through the water.

"*Peste!*" he said. "I don' like! That damn' barometer she's drop to beat hall"

"I sink a storm ees come, *mon capitain*," replied the Haitian. "Borno smell it in ze air."

"Me, I know it too damn' well," said Santos, savagely flinging his cigarette butt overboard. "Another day and we would 'ave made the port, but now—I don' know."

The storm struck two hours later, and so terrific was its force that, despite the fact that every bit of canvas except the jib had been tightly reefed, the foremast cracked and went by the board with the first impact. Santos ordered a small staysail rigged in front of the mainmast, but it was instantly torn to shreds and a seaman was lost.

This threw the ship completely out of control, had any slight measure of control indeed been possible in the swirling, foaming, roaring maelstrom of wind and water that followed.

A helpless plaything of wind and waves, the schooner twisted, turned, rose and plunged, cavorting obediently at the whim of its undisputed master, the storm. The decks were constantly awash, and despite the battened hatches much water leaked into the hold.

Penned in their cage, which was lashed to the mainmast, Jan and Chicma were overwhelmed by wave after wave of seething water. Jan nearly strangled on the first one, but after that learned to do his breathing during the intervals when his head was above water. Chicma seemed to know such things instinctively.

For hour upon hour the storm continued without slackening its violence. Then the forward hatch was ripped off by a huge wave, and water began pouring into the hold.

As suddenly as it had begun, the storm abated, but in the meantime the schooner had shipped so much water she was likely to go down at any minute. Knowing the hand pumps would be useless against this deluge, and feeling his ship sinking beneath his feet, the captain ordered a lifeboat launched, cursing luridly as he took his place in the stern.

EVERY MEMBER of the crew was aboard and the boat was ready to be launched, when Borno who stood in the prow, still wearing his jaguar suit, suddenly leaped back to the, deck.

"Zat boy!" he said. "I mus' turn heem loose!"

"Come back, fool! 'Ave you gone loco?" roared Santos. "We 'ave no time!"

"I mus' save zat boy," replied Borno, whipping his heavy *machete* from his belt as he hurried toward the cage.

"Es wan damn' fool," shouted Santos, to no one in particular. "Lower away."

There was a creaking of davits, a whining of rusty pulleys and the boat splashed to the water. Heavy oars wielded by brawny arms pushed it away from the ship's side. The lifeboat disappeared in the trough of a huge wave, rose on the crest of another, disappeared once more, and was soon far from the ship.

But Borno had not even looked back to note its progress, as intent on his mission of mercy, he chanted a prayer to Ogour Badagris, the Voodoo storm god, and started on his perilous way to the cage. Though still lashed to the mainmast, it had broken some of the ropes and was sliding around on the slippery deck with each lurch of the ship.

Twice the huge Negro was knocked flat by the rushing waters, and twice he regained his feet before he reached his objective. He did not pause to open the wet knots which held the door in place, but slashed them with his *machete*. As he flung the door wide an immense wave swept over the ship and the last lashing broke. The cage, with its two occupants still inside and Borno clinging to one of the bars, was carried overboard.

As the huge wave swept the cage into the seething water, Jan held his breath, hopefully awaiting the opportunity to breathe which had always come in a reasonable length of time before, and clinging to one of the thick bars. But this time it seemed to him that the opportunity would never be forthcoming. His lungs began to hurt; the pain became intense torture. Involuntarily he took a breath, and the torture was magnified a thousandfold as several ounces of salt water rushed into his lungs. Then, blessed relief just in time, the bar to which he was clinging rose above the surface of the water.

Strangling and choking, he inhaled great lungfuls of air. Clinging to a bar beside him, Chicma seemed to be in like case. And swimming beside the floating cage, gripping its door with one huge black hand, Jan saw Borno.

The cage was floating bars up, its opened door swung outward

over the edge and causing one side to sag. Jan tried to climb
out through the door, but before he had half of his body out of
the water the entire cage went under, ducking Chicma. He
subsided into the water once more, and the bars of the cage
emerged. Chicma chattered angrily, and Borno told him to
"Keep down."

Thereafter Jan held his head only above the surface of the
water that sloshed about in the cage. Borno continued swimming with one hand while he held to the door with the other.

Presently Jan heard a roaring sound that seemed familiar.
Then he remembered the sound he had heard shortly before
his first sight of salt water—the roaring of breakers on a beach.
He wanted to raise himself once more to look out, but the
memory of his last experience restrained him.

The roaring grew louder, and great foamy waves began
sweeping over the cage, rocking it violently. Suddenly the
bottom struck something solid, and with its two startled and
half drowned occupants still clinging to the bars, turned over
and over. It stopped with the bars down, half full of water, waves
spanking against one side. Jan and Chicma sat there in the
water, barely able to see the interior of their prison by the dim
light that filtered through the cracks between the planks.

Above the roaring and slapping of the waves Jan heard a
thudding sound. Presently more light came in, and the blade
of Borno's *machete* flashed downward again and again, cutting
a great V in one of the planks. To Jan, sitting there in his soggy
prison, the time seemed interminable before the board was cut
in two.

Borno sheathed his weapon and, seizing a half of the plank,
pulled it toward him, bending the spikes that held it at the
corner. Jan and Chicma quickly squirmed through the opening,
and the three, hurled forward again and again by the breakers
that raced in from behind them, quickly reached a white, sandy
beach.

Apparently exhausted by his efforts, Borno threw himself

on the sand. Chicma, also, squatted on the beach to rest. She was quite old for a chimpanzee, and her recent experience had tired her. But Jan, save for a slight soreness in his lungs and nasal cavities from the salt water: he had inhaled, was feeling not only fit but ravenously hungry.

Just above the matted jungle growth that fringed the beach, three coconut palms reared their crowns, dangling their fruit invitingly. With a wordless cry of delight, Jan plunged through the undergrowth toward them. He was about to spring up the nearest tree, when two powerful brown hands, reaching from behind him, suddenly gripped his throat.

Unable to cry out because of the strangling pressure on his windpipe, Jan was dragged, kicking and struggling, back into the dark depths of the South American jungle.

CHAPTER VII

BROWN MEN'S PRIZE

JAN'S STRUGGLES PRESENTLY grew less as the pressure of the powerful fingers on his throat continued. Then his arms were seized and tightly bound behind his back. For some time he lay on the ground, panting for breath with rattling palate, and staring defiantly up at the strange creature whose prisoner he had become.

The man was short and powerful, and naked save for an abbreviated loin-cloth. His straight black hair was cut in a soup-bowl bob, and his coppery skin glistened with perspiration from his recent exertions, for, despite his youth Jan was stronger than the average man and had given him a good tussle.

Jan watched the native suspiciously as he took up a bundle of long sticks—as long as he was tall—from the ground. One of these sticks was curved, with a string stretched across the curve from tip to tip. The others were sharply pointed at one end. To Jan, a stick had always meant a potential beating, and a low growl rumbled from his throat as his captor made a step toward him.

Puzzled by this unusual sound, coming from a human being, the tall savage paused for a moment, looking quizzically down at his prisoner. He took a second step, and a louder growl resulted. Then he uttered a few words. The youth's only answer was a snarl and a quick leap to his feet. Then he darted into the jungle, his hands still bound behind him.

As he dashed away through the forest, Jan heard a quick

With lightning
swiftness the Indian
struck at Jan's neck.

grunt of surprise. Then there was a_ twang, and one of the long
sticks whizzed past his ear, burying its point in a tree trunk,
where it quivered for a moment as if alive.

Sprinting, leaping, stumbling, dodging first one way, then
another, and constantly goaded to his utmost speed by the
unmistakable sounds of pursuit behind him, the youth ran on
and on until his breath came in great sobbing gasps and there
was a terrific pain in his side: But still the sound of those menacing, footsteps followed him relentlessly, doggedly.

Suddenly there came to his nostrils an odor that was hate-
fully familiar to him. It was the smell of burning wood, and he
instantly associated it with Dr. Bracken and his years of captivity. The cook always burned wood in her kitchen stove, and at
some time during the day there was always a puff of wind to
carry it into the menagerie.

Jan halted for a moment, suspicious of the acrid odor, but a
shout from his pursuer sent him running forward again. The
shout was instantly answered by a voice directly ahead of him.
Soon there were more yells on his right and left, and more
answers from the man who, pursued him. Accompanying the

yells were the patter of footsteps and the rustling of underbrush, warning him that he had been surrounded.

Looking about for a place to hide, Jan selected a clump of huge begonias, which spread their immense leaves nearby. Plunging into this clump, he squatted down, and peering through a space between two gigantic leaves, watched for the approach of the numerous enemies his ears told him were closing in on him.

As he sat there with perspiration streaming from him, endeavoring to keep his labored breathing as quiet as possible, two bronze-skinned savages suddenly came into Jan's line of vision. They passed on, but were succeeded by three more, the last of whom stopped as something caught his attention. It was one of Jan's footprints, and it told this trained hunter as plainly as words that the youth was hidden behind the broad leaves of the begonia. With a loud whoop of exultation, he sprang upon the crouching Jan and dragged him forth.

IN AN instant, Jan was the center of a ring of curious savages, who plucked at his shock of red hair, pulled at his jaguar-skin garment, and poked at his sunburned body as if he were a strange being from another planet, chattering excitedly to each other the while with many grunts and exclamations of amazement.

His spirit unbroken and his anger aroused by this manhandling, Jan voiced his disapproval in the only manner he knew— by alternately snarling and growling at his captors. This demonstration seemed to amuse them hugely, and several of them took to baiting him for the purpose of entertainment.

One huge fellow took it upon himself to poke Jan's tender, sunburned nose with his forefinger. He instantly withdrew the hand with a howl of pain, for Jan, with a quick snap, had bitten it nearly through at the second joint. Enraged, the wounded savage whipped out a *machete* and would have cut off Jan's head, but two companions seized and dragged him away, while the entire party laughed at his discomfiture.

Then Jan's original captor took him by one arm and one of his fellows seized the other, after which they hustled him along between them into a cleared space where a fire was burning and many hammocks were swung. Here Jan's feet were bound, and he was thrown to the ground with one man watching him. Several others gathered around the fire, which they replenished, and over which, when it was going well, they suspended the carcasses of six monkeys, a capybara and two peccaries to roast.

Despite the ache of his bound hands and feet and the stinging bites of numerous tiny black flies, Jan kept every sense alert, listening to the strange chatter of the bronze-skinned men and watching their every movement. All were naked except for their abbreviated loin-cloths, and all were well armed. Some, he observed, had the bent sticks with strings stretched across, and the bundles of sharp-pointed sticks which could fly from them. All had either *machetes* or knives, familiar to Jan because of the assortment of cutlery which Dr. Bracken had used in cutting up meat. Some also carried short, heavy sticks with sharp stones lashed to their thick ends, and some had very long sticks with sharp points.

As soon as they finished eating, the savages, one by one, wandered to their hammocks, which were slung in the smoke of the fire to keep off insect pests and went to sleep.

Jan's original captor brought him some gnawed monkey bones with a little meat left on them, and unbound his hands so he could eat. His fingers were first numb, then filled with a sensation that resembled the pricking of a thousand needles as the blood began to circulate freely in them. He ate a few bites of monkey flesh, took a long drink from a gourd which his captor proffered, and submitted to having his hands bound once more, for he saw that resistance would be useless.

The black flies, which Jan was powerless to brush away, disappeared at nightfall, but their place was taken by hordes of mosquitoes. For hours Jan lay awake squirming and tossing in fruitless endeavor to rid himself of his tiny tormentors But at last he slept.

Awakened at daybreak by a stir in the camp around him, Jan was fed, given a drink of water, and left to watch the preparations for departure. All camp equipment was loaded into a half dozen large baskets, which were carried on men's backs, suspended by broad straps that went around their foreheads. When all was in readiness, Jan's feet were unbound and he was forced to march away with the others.

FOR FIVE days Jan was taken deeper and deeper into the jungle by the band of hunters. Near the end of the fifth day they suddenly emerged into a circular clearing, in the center of which was a large round communal hut or *malocca*, flanked by two crudely constructed lean-tos.

A dozen yapping mongrel dogs rushed out to greet them, instantly followed by more than a score of pot-bellied naked children whose clamor equaled that of the canines, and then by women wearing nothing but small square or triangular aprons.

Jan was dragged to a strong stump about five feet tall near the entrance to the communal hut, and bound to it by strips of fiber passed around his body. Then his hands and feet were unbound and he was given a drink of water. Dogs, children, and women crowded around him, all apparently more curious than the men had been. A dog nipped him on the shin, and Jan promptly kicked it over the heads of the children standing in front. Then a youth of about Jan's age, apparently its master, attempted reprisal by pulling his shock of red hair. Jan cuffed him off his feet with one well-placed blow, much to the young native's chagrin and the amusement of the spectators.

Then a middle-aged matron, evidently the squaw of Jan's original captor, came to his side, knocking children and kicking dogs right and left. After she had cleared a space around him she handed him a piece of something flat and hard, evidently food. He bit into it, finding it rather tasteless and difficult to chew, but it satisfied his hunger which had been developed by the long march. It was a *farinha* cake, made from mandioca root.

Jan was left on exhibition at the stump for some time, but his popularity as an exhibit suddenly waned as another party of hunters returned with a new prisoner whose hands were bound behind him and who was urged forward by spear thrusts from behind. Although, like his captors, he was naked except for a loincloth and copper-skinned, he was much taller than the men who had captured him, none of whom were much taller than Jan, and his aspect was made ferocious by daubs of red ocher on his face, ornamented sections of bamboo thrust through the distended lobes of his ears, and a necklace of jaguar's teeth.

The new prisoner was quickly hustled to the stump and bound like Jan to the opposite side. Women and children crowded around him hurling insults, while dogs barked and snapped at his legs. But despite the abuse heaped upon him, he maintained a stoical silence.

AS THE sun sank lower and lower toward the horizon, and the shadows of the trees that rimmed the clearing grew longer, many children brought firewood, which they heaped around the two who were bound to the post. Jan had no idea what it was for; and although the silent Indian behind him knew, he gave no sign.

A number of cooking fires were built, and much meat was consumed, as both hunting parties had been quite successful. But this time the savages did not retire to their hammocks immediately after their meal. Instead, they formed a large circle around the prisoners.

As soon as darkness fell, Jan's hands were bound like those of the other prisoner, and the circle of spectators began a slow dance around them in time to the throbbing cadence of a kettle-drum beaten by an old man. Many of the dancers carried flaming faggots, snatched from their cook fires, which they thrust into the prisoner's faces or held against their arms or bodies, inflicting painful burns.

Jan struggled to break his bonds, snarling and growling at his tormentors, but to no avail. Presently, imitating his fellow prisoner, who had neither moved nor cried out under torture, he relapsed into silence and ceased his struggles, resolved to show these people that he could stand pain as stoically as the big Indian.

The dance grew faster and faster, the searing thrusts of the lighted faggots more frequent. Then suddenly, as if at a prearranged signal, all of the dancers threw their faggots at the base of the pyre which had been stacked around the two torture victims. Jan heard a crackling sound that swiftly increased in volume. Then there was a sudden upthrust of licking flames and a burst of terrific heat which brought scorching, excruciating agony.

CHAPTER VIII

ORGY

BORNO AND CHICMA did not rest very long on the beach. By the time they were dry from their ocean bath, the rays of the sun had grown intolerable.

The ape got up first, and began sniffing the air as if some far-off scent had attracted her attention. Then she shuffled away in the direction of the jungle.

The big Negro, who was wise in the ways of wild things, observed her actions and followed her. He found her in a small patch of wild pineapples, devouring one of the fragrant fruits. Selecting a ripe one for himself, he drew his *machete* and hacking off the leaves and horny rind, ate it with gusto. As he was about to prepare another he thought of Jan and called him. There was no reply.

"Jan!" he shouted again, with all the power of his huge lungs. But not so much as an echo answered him. Chicma, evidently understanding what was wrong, threw back her head and called to Jan in her barking chimpanzee language.

The big Negro bad been raised in the jungles of his native Haiti, and, it did not take him long after returning to the beach to pick up Jan's trail. Chicma was beside him when he discovered the signs of Jan's struggle, and she bristled up with a snarl.

They followed the trail until nightfall, when darkness made further tracking impossible. Then Borno crept beneath the buttressed roots of a huge *ceiba* tree, and lay down to snatch

44

such sleep as biting insects would allow. The chimpanzee crept in and curled up near him.

In the morning Borno divided his pineapple with Chicma, and they took the trail. Soon they came upon the deserted camp site of the hunters. Toward noon they found a clump of wild bananas and both ate their fill of the fruit. Then Borno shouldered half of a good-sized bunch to take along.

Thus they traveled day by day, Haitian man and African ape, both actuated by the same desire—to rescue the son of a North American millionaire from the savages of a South American jungle.

Near the end of the fifth day, when the man and ape had eaten their evening meal of Brazil nuts, and night had fallen, the hollow booming of a kettledrum came to their ears across the jungle.

Chicma paid no attention to the sound, but when Borno suddenly got up and stole away in the direction of the noise, she followed. The big Negro pushed his way through the jungle as rapidly as possible. Soon he could hear the whoops and yells of the dancers, and the slapping of their bare feet on the packed ground. Then he smelled smoke, saw the flicker of firelight, and emerged into the circular clearing.

Just ahead of him was the huge circle of the community hut. Beside it was the tall stump to which the prisoners were tied, around which the dancers whirled, their faces contorted and hideous in the firelight.

Borno circled and entered the clearing behind the big hut, in order to creep near the fire unobserved. Chicma followed him silently, but when he reached the rear of the *malocca* she sprang up onto its thatched roof.

PAYING NO attention to Chicma, as he did not count on her for much assistance, Borno gripped his heavy cudgel tightly in both hands and dashed around the hut. He had heard the crackle of burning wood which told him' that the death pyre was lighted.

With a blood-curdling yell and a swift rain of bone-crushing blows, he leaped among the dancers felling several and scattering the others right and left. At the same instant Chicma, who had poised herself on the thatched roof just above the door, was dropped inside the hut by the breaking of the roof supports.

The frightened Indians fled in all directions. A few of them started to go into the *malocca* for their weapons. But when they were met at the door by Chicma—a terrifying hairy apparition wearing a jaguar skin, and frothing with rage—they fled weaponless, fully convinced that the evil demons of the jungle had joined forces against them.

Borno, meanwhile, kicked the burning wood away from the post, and with a few deft slashes of his *machete* released both prisoners.

As soon as he was free, the captive Indian rushed into the big hut, emerging with a large bundle of weapons and a big basket of smoked meat. Then he threw several flaming faggots onto the dry thatch, which immediately blazed up, lighting the entire clearing.

"*Vamos!*" he said, with a significant gesture and started away, the basket slung from his brawny shoulders and the weapons carried under one arm.

Borno understood the Spanish word for "Let's go!" and calling to Jan and Chicma, hurried after the tall Indian.

Jan, who had seen the wonderful efficiency of the *machete* paused for a moment to secure one of the coveted weapons from the belt of a fallen savage whose skull had been crushed by the big Negro's cudgel—then followed, with Chicma ambling behind him on hind feet and fore-knuckles.

The Indian, with remarkable precision, struck a narrow, trail at the edge of the clearing. This led them in a short time to a small stream, on the bank of which a number of dugout canoes rested side by side. Into one of these he dropped his basket of smoked meat and bundle of weapons. Then he pushed the other boats, one by one, into the water, permitting them to drift away downstream, while Borno assisted.

When the last empty canoe was drifting downstream, the one which contained the food and weapons was launched, with Jan and Chicma riding in the middle. Borno wielded a paddle in front and the Indian in the rear.

Propelled by the silent strokes of the two powerful men, the canoe shot rapidly downstream, passing, one by one, the empty craft which had already been launched.

Huddled against Chicma, Jan was still suffering much from the burns inflicted by his captors, but he did not whimper nor cry out. Silent and wide-eyed, he drank in the brilliant spectacle of the star-strewn sky reflected by the gently rippling water, and strove to penetrate the mystery of the shadowy banks, from which came many mysterious and terrifying sounds—the night noises of the jungle which he had not learned to interpret.

Steered by the deft paddle of the Indian, the canoe soon emerged into a much broader stream. Here the steersman kept the craft in the middle as if he feared some danger from either shore.

Lulled by the rhythmic strokes of the paddles, Jan fell into a deep slumber and did not awaken until the hot rays of the morning sun struck him full in the face. The canoe was still traveling in the center of the broad river, the two men paddling with unremitting vigor.

THE INDIAN presently steered the canoe toward the left bank. They were almost beneath the overhanging branches and vines before Jan saw that he was making for a narrow inlet, barely wide enough to admit the canoe. A moment more, and they were in the deep shadows beneath the densely matted roof of the jungle. The steersman deftly swung the prow of the boat inshore, and Borno, springing out, dragged it high on the muddy bank while two frightened turtles and a small alligator splashed into the water and disappeared.

Opening the lid of the basket, the Indian took out several

strips of smoked meat. Then he picked up his bundle of weapons and stepped ashore. Depositing the weapons on the ground, he handed a strip of meat to each of his companions and to Chicma. Then he sat down to munch slowly the strip he had kept for himself.

Jan bit into his and found it tough and of a disagreeable flavor. It was tapir meat, hastily cured, and not only had a smoky taste but was rancid. Observing, however, that the Indian devoured his with gusto and that Borno tore off huge mouthfuls with his large white teeth and chewed them with great relish, Jan resolved to eat his whether he liked it or not. But Chicma merely sniffed at hers, then tossed it aside and waddled off into the jungle to look for something more to her liking.

As soon as the Indian had eaten, and drunk from the stream, he promptly stretched out on the ground and went to sleep. Borno followed his example. But Jan, who had slumbered all night in the boat was neither tired nor sleepy. He wandered along the bank of the small stream for a little way, disturbing a number of frogs and turtles, whose splashing leaps into the water interested him, and hacking off shrubs and water plants' with his newly acquired *machete*. This was freedom! This was life, and he gloried in it.

Presently there came a summons from Chicma—the food call. She had found something good to eat, and was calling her foster child to come and share it with her. Interested, but in no great hurry to comply, Jan wandered off in the general direction of the sound, lopping off lianas, branches and bits of bark from tree trunks with his new weapon. It was a fascinating thing, and he wished to become skilled in its use.

Despite his lingering gait, Jan soon arrived within sight of Chicma, who had found a clump of wild orange trees and was hungrily devouring the fruit. But he saw something else which brought a low growl from his throat and caused every hair on his body to stiffen. For, stretched out on a thick limb, his spotted sides barely rising and falling with his suppressed breathing, and the tip of his tail twitching nervously, was Fierce One, the jaguar, apparently about to spring down on the unwary Chicma, who seemed to have no intimation of his presence.

WITH A snarl and a cry of warning which Chicma understood, and which sent her instantly scuttling into a nearby tree, Jan bounded forward.

Surprised and annoyed at this interruption of its hunting, the jaguar turned and with a roar of rage leaped for the youth. The beast was lightning quick, but Jan, who had been trained all his life by a jungle creature, was just a shade quicker. With a slash of his *machete* at the hurtling beast, he flung himself to one side, just out of reach of the raking claws.

The jaguar was swift at recovery, but no swifter than Jan, for as it whirled for a second spring, he was on his feet, his keen *machete* ready for a second cut. In a fleeting instant he saw the result of his previous haphazard slash at his enemy—a paw half severed and dangling uselessly.

Then what had previously been but chance and an instinctive movement of self-protection became a fixed purpose. As the angry brute made its second leap, Jan slashed the other front paw and nimbly eluded the snarling bundle of feline fury. The second blow completely crippled the jaguar's other front paw.

Badly disabled and half disarmed though it was, the fierce beast turned again and attempted a leap. But it was a clumsy effort, and Jan found it easy to step to one side and bring his keen weapon down on the back of the jaguar's neck, severing the vertebrae. With the tenacity of life shown by all members of the cat family, the doomed beast thrashed about for some time, then lay still.

Jan stood back, watching the death struggles of his enemy with some curiosity, alert for a trick. But when the furry form lay quiet, he cautiously advanced and spurned it with his foot. There was no response. He seized a hind leg and turned the great beast over. What made it so limp and helpless? This was the first thing Jan had ever killed, and he did not fully understand it.

Perhaps Fierce One was sleeping, and would presently awaken to attack him. Well, let him come. Jan had overcome the awful alligator, the yellow-bearded man, and now Fierce One. With his tousled red head flung proudly back, he strutted over into the clump of orange trees in search of Chicma.

The old chimpanzee was not there, but by calling to her Jan finally got a reply, far off in the jungle. Chicma would, not come to him, but kept calling him to come with her—that Fierce One would surely eat him. Jan only laughed, but he complied, eventually locating the ape at the top of a tall tree.

"Come down, Chicma," he cried. "Fierce One will not hurt you. He is sleeping."

"It is a trick. He is only waiting to spring upon us," replied Chicma. "We must go farther away from him." Then she caught hold of a huge liana and swung out on it into another tree. By means of the vines and closely matted branches, she made rapid progress which only an ape can make, traveling always in a direction away from the orange grove.

Although he could have followed her with ease among the branches and vines, Jan preferred to walk on the ground. He was filled with pride and the sense of power.

After they got away from the river bank the undergrowth became less matted, so walking was comparatively easy. Jan wanted to show these jungle creatures that he was afraid of none of them.

ALL DAY they traveled through the jungle, Chicma fearfully keeping to the trees while Jan stubbornly remained on the ground. He thoroughly enjoyed the bright-colored butterflies that flapped through the shafts of sunlight, and the gayly plumed, raucous-voiced parrots and macaws.

There was a great flock of monkeys, too, who fled to the topmost branches, chattering vociferously. Jan, who had learned to know and imitate their simian language since infancy, chattered back at them, assuring them of his friendship. But they did not trust him. He looked too much like a man and smelled too much like a jaguar, for the scent of the great cat's blood was still on his *machete* and body. The jaguar skin, too, from which his single garment was fashioned, was a danger signal to jungle dwellers.

Jan regaled himself with the cloying sweetness and fragile beauty of the orchids which grew in great profusion and his heart missed a beat when a huge tapir—much bigger than the jaguar he had killed—came crashing through the jungle in front of him.

It was not until the patches of sunlight no longer penetrated the forest roof and it began to grow dark that Jan thought of Borno and the Indian, sleeping on the muddy bank of the little stream.

He had grown fond of his big black friend, and did not want to desert him. Nor did he want to leave Chicma, who was leading him farther and farther away from the only human being who had unselfishly befriended him.

He stopped and shouted to the chimpanzee to wait. But the cry had scarcely left his lips when something flashed through the forest shadows striking his left side, and spinning him half around with the force of its impact.

Jan clutched at the long shaft, wet with his own blood, and broke it off, gritting his teeth that he might silently bear the pain. Then he reached behind him for that part which had gone through his flesh, and jerked it out. But the pain and loss of blood were too great. A giddiness assailed him, and he sank limply to the ground.

With a whoop of triumph, and *machete* flashing in his hand ready to deliver the death-blow, a savage came bounding out of the shadows.

CHAPTER IX

CHICMA'S ATTACK

SITTING ON A limb fully fifty feet above Jan's head, Chicma heard his call and noticed with bewilderment his actions when the arrow struck him. But when she heard the whoop of the savage, and saw him rushing toward Jan with upraised knife, her mother instinct came to the fore. With a snarl of rage, she swung down from the limb on which she had been sitting, and timed her drop with such precision that she landed on the Indian before he could reach his intended victim.

Knocked off his feet by the impact of the hairy body of the ape, the Indian fell on his face, dropping both his *machete* and his longbow. For a moment he lay there, half stunned and breathless. Then Chicma sank her huge teeth into his neck. The pain brought him to his senses, and he groped for his weapons. Failing to find them; he stood up and shook himself with the ape still clinging to him like a bloodthirsty octopus.

Watching the struggle of the two as through a dim haze, Jan made several attempts to rise, but each time fell back because of the giddiness induced by his wound. It was not until he saw the Indian stoop and reach for his *machete* that he was able to get to his feet.

His keen weapon recovered, the savage made a slash at Chicma's head. She dodged, and he was about to swing for her again when he saw Jan facing him, similarly armed. With light-ning swiftness he struck for the youth's neck, a blow so power-ful that it would have severed his head from his body. But Jan

52

was faster than the savage, even though giddy. Avoiding the deadly blow by a quick step backward, he leaped in before the red man could recover. Jan's *machete* flashed once, and the Indian's hand, still clutching his weapon, flew into the undergrowth. Jan's blade flashed a second time and the savage fell to the ground with a fatal body wound, and died almost at once.

Jan gathered up the weapons of his fallen foe: a bow, a bundle of arrows, and a *machete* with belt and case. Then he and Chicma proceeded on through the forest. His wound was very painful, but not dangerous as the arrow had passed only through the muscles beneath his left arm without injuring any vital organs. When darkness came on, with the suddenness of the tropics, they perched themselves, supperless, in a tall tree for the night.

RISING WITH the sun the youth and the ape set out in search of breakfast and a drink of water. But it was not until half the day had passed that they found either. Then, suddenly emerging from the depths of the tangled jungle, they came upon both in satisfying abundance. They found themselves on the bank of a tiny stream, the water of which was clear and cold. Growing on both banks of this stream in profusion were oranges, pineapples and bananas.

Having drunk their fill of the sparkling water and satisfied their appetites with the fruit, they proceeded along the bank of the little stream. They had not gone far before Jan heard, ahead of them, a strange noise that made him uneasy. He looked quickly at Chicma to see if it had alarmed her, but she plodded along so unconcernedly that he decided it could not be anything of consequence.

The noise grew louder as they proceeded, until they came to a sheer cliff of bare rock towering more than two thousand feet above the jungle. Emerging from a hole in this rock about fifty feet above the level of the stream, was a small waterfall. Clear and limpid as crystal, it tumbled almost vertically into an oval pool.

Jan gasped with admiration at the beauty of this scene. He

tried to explain his feelings to Chicma, but being tired and sleepy she only grunted and climbed a tall tree beside the pool to find a comfortable crotch for a nap. To her this was merely a place where food and drink might be had in abundance. Until the food gave out or the place became too dangerous here she would remain.

While Chicma took her nap, Jan practiced with his new weapons. While a prisoner of the hunters, he had often seen them use the bent stick with the string stretched across it. He found however, that it was far from being as easy as it looked. The bow was stiff, requiring all his strength to bend it, and the arrows seemed to strike anywhere but the place intended.

With the passing days, however, he mastered the weapon, though he had lost or broken most of his arrows in the meantime.

Chicma spent the greater part of her time dozing in the tree, only coming down for food or water, but Jan, always searching for something new, roamed away from the pool every day. For a long time he subsisted only on fruit, as did the ape, but growing within him, day by day, was the desire for meat, his favorite food.

One day he brought down a curassow with one of his arrows. Curious he cut into it with his *machete*. A slab of the turkey-like breast meat came away, and Jan, who had never tasted other than raw meat before his escape from Dr. Bracken, sampled it. Finding it good, he cut away and ate as much as he wanted, then took the rest back to the pool with him, hanging it in the tree to keep. But in the morning when he awoke, ravenous after his long sleep, he found it swarming with little white worms and giving forth an abominable stench. Disgusted, he hurled it far out into the jungle, and set forth after new meat.

The first animal to cross his path was an ocelot, the beautiful markings of which gave him the impression that its flesh must be delicious. Having wounded it with an arrow, he foolishly rushed to close quarters to finish it with his *machete*. But the fierce tiger cat, sorely wounded though it was, gave him a terrific battle, from which he did not fully recover for two weeks. And its meat, he found, was not nearly so good to eat as that of the dingy-colored curassow.

Day by day the youth learned the lessons that the jungle had to teach him. He learned to hunt with the silence and cunning of the jaguar, to travel among the branches and vines with the ease and facility of the monkeys, or to speed along the forest floor with the swiftness of the deer and the stealth of the panther.

Man, he found, was his natural enemy, and after several encounters in which he barely escaped with his life, he took to stalking the savages as he would jaguars or ocelots. Only a few escaped with their lives to tell of a red-headed jungle demon, half man, half jaguar, that shot at them from the trees and made off through the branches as easily as a monkey.

AFTER TWO years he had not only learned many of the hardest lessons which the jungle has to teach, but had accumulated a small arsenal of weapons taken from the savages he had slain. There were a score of bows, more than a hundred arrows, a dozen long spears, five blow-guns with their deadly poison-tipped darts, and a miscellaneous assortment of steel and stone axes, *machetes*, knives, ornaments and trappings.

He had watched the birds building their nests and the natives their huts; and the idea had come to him to combine the two in the big tree in which he and Chicma slept. It proved a hard task indeed for his untutored hands, but after nearly a month of trials and tearings down, he completed a round, compact, rainproof tree—but about fifty feet above the ground, divided into two parts by a rude partition. On the floor of each "room" he made a nest of soft grass. The hut proved snug and dry, even during the heaviest of the tropical rains.

In this hut he kept his weapons, ornaments and other treasures—bits of bright stone that he had picked up, teeth, claws, and sometimes bones of animals he had slain, bright feathers and plumes from the birds he had brought down, and a few odorous, badly cured hides.

Very often he bored Chicma by repeating the human words which Borno had taught him.

All this time he felt stirrings and yearnings for which he could not account. He was not content to make short journeys from the hut, returning at nightfall, but took to wandering farther and farther away, sleeping in the trees at night. He was always discontented—searching for something, he knew not what, but always searching, always going farther and remaining away longer.

ONE MORNING when he was four days' journey from the hut, he suddenly emerged from the jungle into a grove of trees that appeared most strange and unnatural to him. They grew in straight rows, evenly spaced almost to the very edge of a broad river. There was little undergrowth beneath them, and no rope-like lianas were draped among their branches.

Jan was puzzled. Stealthily he moved forward among the slender, straight trunks to investigate this unusual place. But he had riot gone more than a few steps before he saw something that caused him to stop and hastily dodge behind one of the tree trunks. To Jan, all strange humans were enemies, and he instinctively fitted a long arrow to his bowstring. But as he gazed at the creature coming toward him, something held his hand. This being was unlike any he had ever seen before and more lovely than the fairest jungle flower that had ever charmed his innate sense of beauty.

He gazed, spellbound, while the wonderous creature sat down on the moss beneath one of the trees, and leaning against it, opened what he thought was a basket of white leaves on which there were many strange little black tracks. Curious as he was about the basket with white leaves, he could not keep his eyes off the face above it. The being had dark-brown hair, as curly as Jan's own, tumbling just below the nape of a snow-white neck. The big brown eyes were half-veiled by the long, curling lashes, pink cheeks, and a tiny red mouth.

This creature, Jan thought, looked altogether too fragile to be dangerous and was, moreover, too beautiful to be destroyed. He relaxed his bowstring and was about to lower his arrow, when he suddenly caught sight of something which caused him to bring the arrow quickly back to the firing position. It was the flash, through a brilliant patch of sunlight, of a tawny, stealthily moving creature, larger than a jaguar and more formidable. The only beast in the menagerie which had resembled it was Terrible One, the lion, so Jan instinctively thought of it in those terms.

As the puma, a giant of his species, crept closer and closer, Jan, who had watched the hunting of these great cats many times in the jungle, became aware that it was stalking the lovely human he had been admiring. He could see the tip of the long, yellow tail twitching, the mighty muscles preparing for the swift charge which even the fastest of the jungle creatures seldom escapes. Jan foresaw the outcome—a lightning leap, a rending, bone-crushing blow from the huge paw, a crunch of the mighty jaws, and a limp and bloody victim being dragged away to some jungle lair to be devoured.

Many times Jan had seen these great cats bring down their prey, and never had he intervened to save the victim. But this victim was different. He could not bear to see that beauty marred—that frail body mangled and bleeding. Drawing the arrow back with all his strength, he took careful aim at the tawny shoulder, and let fly.

The arrow flew true to the mark, and the great carnivore, with a terrific roar of rage and pain, sprang out of its hiding place, straight for the girl it had marked for its prey.

But quick as was the puma, Jan was there before it, barring the way. His bow and arrows he had tossed aside, and his keen *machete* gleamed in his hand. Snarling furiously, the immense beast reared up on its hind legs—taller by a head than Jan—and slapped at him with a mighty paw. Jan dodged to one side, nearly severing the paw with his *machete* as he did so; and he would have been temporarily out of danger in another instant, had not his toe caught on a root, sending him sprawling.

Before he could make another move'the puma pounced upon him, sinking its great teeth into his left shoulder, shaking him as a cat shakes a mouse, and raking and gouging him with its terrible, sickle-like claws.

The youth felt his strength waning fast. He tried to use big *machete*, but his efforts seemed feeble, futile. He backed at the side of the monster's head again and again, cutting off an ear, blinding an eye, leaving nothing on one side but a bloody mass of mangled flesh and bone. But the powerful jaws would not relax their hold. The bulging; muscular neck continued to pivot that gory head as it swiftly shook Jan's limp body.

Jan had reached the limit of human endurance. It seemed to him that a great weight was crushing him, forcing the breath from his body. His *machete* dropped from his nerveless fingers, and merciful unconsciousness crept over him.

CHAPTER X

OUTSIDE THE WALLS

AT SIXTEEN RAMONA SUAREZ was still something of a tomboy. She loved to mingle with the dark-skinned children and mongrel dogs of the laborers on her father's great rubber plantation. She took great delight in climbing trees, scaling walls and exploring thickets, to the despair of her doting old duenna, Señora Soledade. Her duenna scolded her, her mother, Doña Isabella, tried to reason with her, and her father, Don Fernando, who secretly chuckled over her escapades, tried to look stern when required to lecture her.

But they might as profitably have scolded the wind, reasoned with the rain cloud, or lectured the lightning. Ramona would listen dutifully, then, with a flash of white teeth and a shake of her dark brown ringlets; would romp away to hatch up some new deviltry.

Señora Soledade, corpulent and dignified, was of the opinion that the big patio, with its flowers shrubs and trees, winding walks; vine-clad arbors and bubbling fountains, was a large enough world for any girl. Charged with the duty of keeping Ramona always in sight, and taking the task in all seriousness, she was really able to do so only about half the time.

One day the old duenna was seated in the shade of an arbor in the patio, working on a bit of lace, and Ramona was busily engaged beneath a nearby orange tree with her English tutor, Arthur Morrison. Quite positive that her charge would not get away so long as the tutor was about, and drowsy from the mounting heat, the *señora* settled back comfortably in her chair, and with her hands folded over her ample equator, dozed.

But scarcely had she fallen asleep when the tutor, with a final charge to his pupil to study diligently, strolled away.

Ramona waited slyly until the tutor had entered the house. Then she peeked at the old lady, and saw that the coast was clear. Leaving her text-books, pencils and rulers beneath the orange tree, she picked up one of her favorite story books and climbed the tree.

At first it had been Ramona's intention to read the book in the tree, thus dumfounding the duenna when she should awaken; yet one side of the tree overhung the patio wall, giving her a new idea. Softly she let herself down from, a branch to the top of the wall, then, with the book gripped between her teeth, suspended herself by her hands on the other side, and dropped. She had attained the freedom she craved and she meant to make the most of it.

Tucking the book under her arm, she wandered off between the tall straight trunks of one of her father's young rubber groves until she came to the river bank. Then she sat down, leaned against a tree, and immersed herself in her book.

Ramona was an avid reader, and soon forgot her surroundings. But she was brought sharply back to reality by two sounds, one following the other in rapid succession: the twang of a bow-string and the roar of a mountain lion. For a moment she was paralyzed with fear and in that moment the great beast charged:

But quick as the puma had been, there was one who was quicker. Ramona was conscious for an instant of the lithe, auburn-haired youth who put himself between her and the charging death. Then for a moment things happened so swiftly that she could scarcely follow them—the roaring beast, the youth's swift and skillful slash that crippled one of the great paws, and his leap for safety, blocked by the projecting root.

The girl uttered a single, piercing scream as she saw her

champion go down. Then she leaped to her feet, undecided for a moment whether to run for help or go to the assistance of her champion. She decided on the latter course, and looked around for a weapon.

JAN'S BOW and arrows lay where he had thrown them, and she caught them up. Fitting an arrow to the string, she aimed it at the heaving flank of the puma, and pulled. But the hardwood bow was very stiff, and even though Ramona exerted her utmost strength she could only draw the arrow back a few inches. As a result, it barely penetrated the tough skin with little more effect than the bite of a fly.

Seeing the futility of that, Ramona struck at the puma with the heavy bow. But here, again her strength was not great enough to distract the attention of the huge feline. What could she do to save this handsome knight of the jungle who had come so gallantly to her rescue?

She knew that house-cats become greatly annoyed when their tails are pulled. Perhaps this also applied to the big cats of the jungle. She could only try.

Springing around to the rear, she seized the long tail with both hands, braced her feet, and pulled. At this instant, the snarling of the beast was stilled. She saw the *machete* fall from Jan's fingers—saw him go limp at the same moment that the puma, a final shiver running through its frame, sank heavily down on his senseless body.

Ramona leaped to one side and pulled. Gradually she was able to drag the great beast off the prostrate form of her champion. But the sharp teeth were still clamped into the bloody and lacerated shoulder. Picking up the *machete,* she pried the jaws apart.

Tenderly she raised the youth's head, placed it in her lap, and with her tiny handkerchief attempted to wipe away the blood. But the little square of lace proved quite inadequate, and she threw it away, soaked with blood, before more than a small part of one cheek had been cleansed.

The river was only about twenty feet away. Gently lowering his head from her lap, she dragged him to the water's edge. She ripped a panel of cloth from her white frock, and dipping it in the water, proceeded to bathe his face and wounded shoulder.

The cold water and the pressure of the cloth on Jan's wounds brought him to his senses. The blinding pain made him think for a moment that he was still in the grip of the puma. He tried to escape. Springing erect he knocked his little nurse flat in the mud.

For a moment he stood there, staring wildly down at her, while she gazed back in wide-eyed wonder and alarm. Then she smiled, a wistful little smile, and Jan, who in all the jungle had found no friends save Chicma and Borno, knew that he had found another.

He wanted to say something to her. But what? And how? It would be useless to bark at her in the chimpanzee language. He had tried that unsuccessfully on Borno and other humans. And the few words which Borno had taught him had quite vague meanings for him. However, they were human words, and this creature was undoubtedly human.

"I spik ze Engleesh," he announced, with Borno's accent, intently watching to see what effect his words would have.

She smiled again, and sprang lightly to her feet.

"I speak it, too," she said. "My name is Ramona."

"My name Jan," he replied, and added naively, "Jan like you."

Before the girl, could reply the shrill voice of Señora Soledade called:

"Ramona!"

"*Sí, señora,*" she replied.

"Come here this instant!" was the command in Spanish, which of course Jan did not understand.

"I must go now, Jan. Good-bye," said Ramona, and ran through the grove in the direction from which the voice had come.

Jan watched her until she disappeared from view. Then, with

strange reluctance, he picked up his *machete* and his bow and arrows, and plunged off into the jungle. His wounds were very painful, especially his mangled shoulder. He must get to Chicma as soon as possible. She would lick them and make them well after the manner of ape mothers, as she had often licked the bloody welts inflicted by Cruel One, the doctor. But he was hot thinking of his wounds.

IT HAD taken him only four days to reach the rubber plantation from their tree-hut, but that was when he was well and strong. Wounded and weakened by loss of blood, he was six days in making the return journey. By this time his wounds had closed and although they were still quite painful, Chicma showed no interest in them.

Recalling the soothing effect of the water with which Ramona had bathed his hurts he left the chimpanzee dozing in the tree-hut and, descending, waded into the pool beneath the waterfall. The cold water allayed the fever, and he paddled about for some time in the manner of a young puppy.

For two more weeks he divided his time between the tree-hut and the pool, doing no hunting, and living on the fruits that abounded in, this earthly paradise. One day, as he was paddling and splashing in the water, he discovered that by moving his hands and feet in a certain way he could keep afloat. Thrilled by this discovery, he tried again and again, until he was able to swim about the pool at will.

Interested in this new sport, he began to watch the manner in which other creatures of the jungle swam, and to imitate them. The four-legged animals, he noticed swam as he did, but the frogs did it in quite a different fashion. It was some time before he was able to duplicate their kicking stroke, but he mastered it eventually.

The frogs, he decided, were the really expert water creatures, and he attempted to imitate them further by entering the water as they did. His first dive was not a pronounced success, as forgetting his lesson on the ocean, he made the mistake of trying to breathe beneath the surface. Half-strangled, he quickly paddled to shore, and having coughed up most of the water, decided to try again.

It was not long before he learned to hold his breath and dive with the swift skill of the amphibians.

At first he only dived off the bank of the pool, but later he began practicing dives from higher points—a projecting ledge of rock, an overhanging limb. Once his foot slipped and he fell from a considerable height, alighting flat with a loud smack that all but knocked the wind from him. This taught him that the water could be very soft or very hard, according to the way one fell. After that, he took care to cleave it cleanly and gracefully.

One day, when his wounds were healed and he was beginning to feel the urge of the jungle trails, he dived from one of the lower boughs of the tree in which his hut was situated. The force of the dive carried him clear up behind the curtain of tumbling waters—a place he had not previously explored. He drew himself up onto a jagged, rocky ledge and sat there for some time, listening to the roar of the falls and admiring the thin sheet of water with the faint light filtering through it.

Presently, as his eyes became accustomed to the dim light of the place, he made out, high above him, two figures so strikingly manlike in form that he started and involuntarily clutched the hilt of his sheathed *machete*—without which he seldom ventured anywhere. In a moment he saw that they were not men, but harmless images of stone with manlike bodies and grotesque faces, one of which resembled that of a hawk, and the other that of a dog. He also noticed that leading up the face of the cliff to the ledge on which they stood, were a number of notches cut deeply into the stone.

SPRINGING TO his feet, he climbed rapidly upward by means of the notches, and drew himself up on the ledge. Here a new surprise awaited him, for he saw that the two grotesque statues guarded the mouth of a dark passageway which extended into the solid rock beneath the waterfall.

His curiosity aroused, Jan cautiously entered the passageway. It led straight into the cliff for about fifteen feet, then veered to the right and upward. As soon as he made the turn, he was in total darkness and was compelled to grope his way forward.

The passageway leveled out, presently, and turned sharply to the left.

Still groping in inky blackness, Jan discovered, by the murmur of water beside the pathway, that he was walking on the bank of an underground stream. A walk of about ten minutes brought him to a point where dim light filtered into the cavern. It came from just above the surface of the water, where the cavern roof dipped, arching over it at a height of only a few inches. Here the path he had been following led straight into the water.

Jan paused here for a moment undecided whether to go on or to retrace his steps. But his insatiable curiosity won out and he waded into the water. The bank sloped steeply, and he was soon swimming against the swift current.

When he reached the point from which the light emanated he was forced to turn on his back in order to keep his nose above water, because of the narrow space between the cavern roof and the surface of the stream.

Suddenly he shot out into the bright sunlight. Turning over, he looked about him and saw that he was in the middle of a narrow river, which apparently flowed straight into the solid rock. A few swift strokes took him to shore. He climbed the high bank, and when he reached the top, stopped in sudden amazement at what he saw. For he stood before the ruins of an immense building, the remaining walls of which were covered with gigantic bas-reliefs depicting strange, angular-looking human beings, some with heads like birds or animals, some with beards that reminded him of the detested Dr. Bracken, and some with not unhandsome human features. They seemed to be engaged in fighting each other, or in hunting strange beasts or birds.

Some of the tall columns of the facade were still standing, supporting fragments of ornamental cornices. Others had fallen and broken into cylindrical sections.

Guarding the portal of this strange edifice, on either side, were two colossal statues with bodies that were human in form, but one had a face like a hawk's and the other like that of a dog. They resembled the two statues he had seen beneath the waterfall, but were much larger.

Leading to this portal were the remains of a paved avenue now broken and weed-grown. Along each side of this highway was a row of pedestals, on some of which stood statues of grotesque monster, half beast, half human. Others had fallen or been overturned, and their cracked and shattered fragments were strewn about among the weeds and broken fragments of paving slabs.

Thrilled with awe and wonder at these strange sights, Jan was slowly advancing toward the portal when he caught the guarded movement of something creeping toward him in the undergrowth at his right. He whipped out his *machete* and paused, watching breathlessly. Then he saw another movement as something passed through the undergrowth on his left.

Suddenly two great shaggy creatures bounded out onto the sparsely grown avenue and closed in on him. They were manlike and yet apelike in form with long bushy beards and hairy bodies. One brandished a huge club menacingly, while the other hurled a large rock fragment straight at the boy's head.

Jan managed to dodge the missile, and turned to flee. But he had not taken more than a dozen leaps when a third hairy monster sprang in front of him, barring his progress, and swung for his head with a heavy cudgel.

CHAPTER XI

THE JUNGLE DEMON

WHEN SHE SAW the bedraggled and blood-soaked condition of her charge, Ramona's old duenna threw up her hands and shrieked in holy terror. Ramona's dress was smeared with mud in the back and with blood in front The cloth which she had ripped away to use for binding Jan's wounds left a rent that exposed the peach-tinted silk clinging to her trim little figure, which was also considerably spotted with gore.

Don Fernando, who had been walking in the patio nearby, smoking one of his long, slim cigars, came dashing up just as Señora Soledade swooned away.

"*Carramba!*" he exclaimed, dropping his cigar and catching Ramona in his arms, to the detriment of his immaculate white suit. "Tell me what has happened, my little one! Where are you hurt?"

"I'm not hurt, daddy," replied Ramona, "but Señora Soledade has fainted."

"Not hurt! But this blood! These soiled, torn clothes! I don't understand!"

"It is not my blood, daddy. It's Jan's. He saved me from the puma."

"*Madre de Dios!* Jan? The puma? What is all this? Tell me, quickly, or I, too, shall collapse!"

"But first let us attend the *señora*."

At this moment, Señora Soledade sat up and gazed wildly about her.

67

Don Fernando stood his daughter on her feet, and gallantly hurried forward to help the old lady. But when she saw the blood on his white suit she shrieked, and seemed about to swoon again.

"Come, come," he said. "Be brave. Ramona is all right and so am I."

"But the blood! The—"

"There, there!"

He piloted her gently through the patio gate, seated her on a bench, and returned.

"Now child," he said. "This puma. This Jan. Tell me about them."

"Come with me and I'll show you the puma," she answered. "It's dead."

She related the story of her adventure to her father, as she led him to where the dead carnivore lay. Don Fernando listened gravely to her story, and examined the fallen feline with interest.

"A giant of its kind, that beast," he said. "A terrible foe. And you say it was slain by a mere boy?"

"I didn't say a *mere* boy," replied Ramona reprovingly. "He was magnificent."

"Yes, of course my little one. A gallant knight who came to your rescue. But for him I would have lost you." He threw his arm around her and drew her close. "I wish I could reward him."

"And why can't you?"

"Your description of him…. Do you know who he is?"

"To be sure. He is Jan. He told me so."

"Yes, but your description of him: red hair, a garment of jaguar skin. He is the wild boy who has slain so many natives during the past two years. Many strange tales have been told about him. When first seen he had two companions—a giant black man and a great hairy ape. Both of these wore jaguar-skin garments, also. They terrorized a small Indian community,

*With jaws gaping,
the serpent struck.*

killing several. Since then the boy has been seen once or twice
with the great ape, but mostly he travels alone. No one knows
what has become of the black giant. Do you know what they
call this boy?"

"No."

"They call him the jungle Demon. Some say he is half man,
half jaguar. He travels with equal facility on the ground or
through the tree tops. When an Indian is found dead, stripped
of his weapons and ornaments, they say: 'It is the jungle Demon
again.' He is more fierce, more terrible and more dangerous
than the puma he has slain. All men are his enemies."

"But he said he liked me."

"*Carramba!* Did he? Then promise me this: that you will
never leave the house or patio again unless I or one of the men
go with you, armed. Some day he will come to steal you—to
carry you off to his jungle lair to a horrible fate. It would be a
terrible blow to your mother and me, and to poor old Señora
Soledade. Won't you do this much for us? Won't you promise?"

Don Fernando had long since learned that threats or com-
mands meant nothing to Ramona, but that she could be ap-

pealed to in a reasonable manner, and that if she made a promise, that promise would be carried out.

"I don't know, daddy," she answered. "I so love to get away by myself once in a while."

"Yes, I know. But think of the danger. And think of your mother and father, and of your old duenna, who loves you."

"All right daddy, I'll promise."

And so they went into the patio, arm in arm.

AS THE first man-monster of the ruined temple struck at him with his cudgel, Jan, who had often dodged the swift blow of a jaguar's paw, easily eluded his clumsy swing. The force of the blow turned the hairy one part way around. Jan leaped in and dealt him a blow on the back of his neck with the keen *machete*. The monster fell on his face without a sound, his spinal column severed by the sharp blade.

With savage yells the other two closed in to avenge their fallen comrade, but Jan was already running swiftly toward the river.

Sheathing his weapon, he sprang from the top of the bank, in a long, graceful dive. He swam frog-like beneath the surface until a shadow above him told him that he had entered the underground channel. Then he arose and, turning on his back, inhaled the welcome air.

As he drew himself up on the bank in the semi-darkness, he hesitated for a moment. These men were deadly enemies. Being bearded like Dr. Bracken and the brutal Jake Grubb on the ship, they were doubly hateful. He wanted to go back—to stalk and slay them.

But the jungle, his jungle, was calling. Already he was longing to swing through its sun-dappled branches and lianas again, and tread the soft leaf mold in its deeper shadows. And beyond the jungle was a beautiful being—Ramona.

Jan groped his way back to the falls. Then he descended the notched cut in the cliff, dived through the curtain of water into the pool, and came up beneath his tree-hut. Shaking the water from his glistening body, he climbed up and found Chicma dozing peacefully in her compartment. She gave a little grunt of greeting as he looked in, then went to sleep once more.

As time went on she had been paying less and less attention to his comings and goings. No longer did she romp with him in mimic combat, or play at tag with him through the tree tops. She liked her soft nest, and rarely left it except when urged by hunger or thirst. Chicma was getting very old.

Jan took up his favorite bow and a well-filled quiver of arrows, and left. As he plunged into his jungle, it was good to feel the soft leaf mold under his bare feet, the cool leaves brushing against his face and body.

He was meat-hungry, and his archery soon won him an unwary curassow. Having eaten, he hurried onward with a fixed purpose—to reach, as soon as possible, the place where he had found Ramona. With Borno gone and Chicma become grouchy and unsociable, he longed for the companionship of a friend. And Ramona was the only other living creature who had shown friendship for him.

She attracted him, too, in a different way from the others. At thought of her his pulse would quicken in a manner quite impossible to explain.

He shortened what had been a four-day journey to three. Arriving at the edge of Don Fernando's grove of young rubber trees, he hurried to the place where he had last seen her. But he found only the gnawed bones of the puma.

Recalling the direction in which she had gone when called, he went that way and eventually arrived at the patio gate. It was made from heavy planks which fitted a high-arched gateway. He looked through a crack between two planks and saw the object of his quest, seated beneath a tree and holding before her the basket of white leaves with little black tracks on them.

Jan knew nothing of the mechanism of the gate, and the smooth, plastered surface of the high patio wall offered no opportunity for a finger hold, but he observed that a branch of the tree under which the girl was sitting overhung the wall near a branch of a rubber tree outside. This made a clear path for the jungle-trained Jan.

HEARING A slight sound in the tree above her, Ramona was about to cry out in fear, but she stifled the sound when her knight-errant dropped softly beside her.

"Jan!" she whispered. "You startled me!"

"Come see you," he responded. "Jan like you."

"Shh! Not so loud. You will wake my duenna."

"Jan don' understan'," he said, imitating her low tones.

She rose, and drew aside the branch of a bushy shrub, one of a clump. Just behind it he saw a short and very round woman in black, seated in a gaudily striped lawn chair with her hands folded in her lap, snoring quite audibly. The thought flashed to his mind that this must be some deadly enemy of Ramona's. With a low growl he whipped his bow and arrow from the quiver, and took quick aim at the old lady.

The horrified girl caught his hand.

"No, no! You must not hurt her! She is my friend. She loves me. But she must not know that you are here with me."

Puzzled, the youth replaced bow and arrow in his quiver.

"Jan try understan'," he whispered.

She laid a hand on his arm.

"Sit here beside me," she said, "so you will not be seen. Then, if we talk quietly, no one will know that you are here, and perhaps you may come again."

They talked for nearly half an hour, Jan asking questions in his limited broken English aided by the universal language of signs and Ramona trying to explain things to him. He asked her about the little basket of white leaves covered with many black tracks, and she told him the little tracks talked to her. She told him the basket was called a "book," and that the tracks were called "letters," while groups of tracks were called "words."

At the end of a half hour Ramona said:

"You must go now, Jan. As soon as Señora Soledade finishes her siesta she will look for me and I don't want her to see you. Come tomorrow at this time, and I will be here."

Jan left without protest, going over the wall as he had come. Once in the jungle, he shot a peccary, ate his fill, drank deeply at the river, and crept beneath the roots of a *ceiba* to dream of a pair of lustrous brown eyes.

And Ramona, having sent him away, was thrilled by her power over this handsome youth who, though he was a mighty slayer of fierce beasts and savage men, obeyed her, lightest request without question.

CHAPTER XII

IN A SERPENT'S COILS

ON THE FOLLOWING day, and for many days thereafter, Jan met Ramona beneath the tree in the garden. As she had made it plain that she did not want these meetings known, he always came and went with the utmost caution. The hollow beneath the roots of the *ceiba* tree became his home. The fruit and game of the nearby jungle supplied him with ample food.

On the second day, Don Fernando, walking in the patio with his spotless white suit and smoking his long, slim cigar, had a narrow escape from death when Ramona stopped Jan just in time as he was preparing to launch an arrow. Gradually she was able to make him understand, how dear her father, mother and duenna were to her, and that her tutor and the servants were friends who must not be slain or injured.

Much of the time she spent in tutoring him. Jan was an eager pupil, and mastered the alphabet in a few days. Then he tackled an English reader. Ramona's parents, having been educated in the United States, she was able to correct Jan's accent.

He was particularly interested in her books on natural history. Many animals he recognized at once by their pictures, having seen them in the jungle. He marveled at the pictures of the mighty prehistoric monsters, saying he wished he could meet and overcome some of them in battle. He was quite disappointed when Ramona told him they were all dead.

Jan was greatly attracted, too, by Ramona's writing and drawing materials. For many days, he watched her sketch. Then, one day, she gave him pencil, paper, and drawing board, and found that, without training, he could do almost as well as she. His greatest delight was to copy the pictures in the natural history books, labeling each sketch with its correct name which, having once learned, he never forgot.

Each day Jan brought some offering from the jungle for his little goddess. He sought out the rarest orchids and the most luscious fruits and berries. Once, after art encounter with a Carib native, he brought her a necklace of jaguar teeth. But she did not dare to keep it, much to his disappointment.

Jan noticed that she had in the palm of her right hand, a blue tracing of a many-petaled flower. One day, with pen and ink, he traced a similar flower in his own palm. But to his surprise, the ink soon rubbed off. He tried to find out what made hers stay, but she, didn't know. The mark had been there always—as long as she could remember.

One afternoon Jan was drawing, using a sharp, flexible pen and India ink, when he accidentally pricked his finger. The next morning he noticed a little blue spot where the wound had been. When, after a lapse of several days, the spot remained, he began to trace a blue flower in his own palm in this manner. The work took some time, and cost him a sore hand for a while, but he ended by having a permanent tattoo mark almost identical with that of Ramona, and was delighted with the result.

As soon as he had learned sufficient English, Jan told Ramona about his early life in the menagerie, and of Dr. Bracken, whom he called "Cruel One." He was amazed and deeply relieved when Ramona told him that it was impossible for Chicma to have been his mother. He often wondered after that what his real mother was like, and if he would ever see her.

FOR MORE than two months, Jan lived beneath the *ceiba* near the plantation, watching the rubber workers, the house servants, and Ramona's parents and friends, and stealing in to see her at every opportunity.

To Ramona these secret meetings with her jungle hero were

delightfully romantic. She felt a little remorseful about them at first, knowing that her parents would not approve. But she had only promised her father that she would not leave the house or the patio alone, and this promise was being carried out to the letter.

When she had progressed sufficiently with her studies, her parents planned to send her to the United States, then to Europe, to complete her education. At the end of the two-month period of Jan's stay the time for her departure was near at hand. He noticed a change in her and asked what was wrong, but she would not tell him until the last day.

As she was helping him with his reading lesson, a tear suddenly splashed on the page. Jan looked at her in surprise.

"What is the matter?" he asked. "Why do you cry?"

"I'm going away for a long time," she said. "I may never see you again."

"If you go away I will follow," he replied.

"You must not try to follow," she said. "You could only go along for a little way, anyhow. First we will travel down the river in some of my father's small boats. We will go around the rapids, several of them, the Indians carrying the boats and luggage. Then we will take a small steamer. This steamer will carry us to a seaport where we will take a bigger one that will take us across the ocean, far, far from here. Many thousands of miles."

"But won't you come back?"

"I hope to, some day. But it will be a long time."

"I will wait and watch for you," said Jan.

He stood up and slung his quiver over his shoulder. There was a heavy weight in his breast, and something was choking him.

Suddenly Ramona stood on tiptoes, threw her arms around his neck and kissed him.

"Good-bye," she whispered. "Wait for me, and I'll wait for you."

Then she darted off through the shrubbery, light-footed as a young deer.

To Jan, who had never before been kissed, who had not known there was such a thing, it was a most astounding and pleasant experience. For a moment he stood in a daze, gazing after the fleeing girl. Then he scampered up the tree, swung out on the limb, and dropped to the ground beyond the patio wall.

At last his preoccupied mind thought of Chicma, and he felt a twinge of remorse at having neglected her so long. No knowing what might have happened to her. Plunging into the jungle, he resolved to go straight to his tree-hut. Never before had he been separated from Chicma for so long, and though the old comradeship had dwindled, he could never forget the tender care she had given him, nor the many romps they had taken together. He was very sad and lonely, and his mind was filled with gloomy forebodings.

As fast as he had hurried away from the hut, he hurried back.

Late in the afternoon of the third day, he reached his objective. He peered into the hut and called softly in the language of the chimpanzees.

There was no answer. The hut was deserted.

Alarmed, he swung out on one of the upper limbs and called again, as loudly as he could shout.

He was surprised and delighted when the answer came back from almost directly beneath him. Chicma was waddling unconcernedly along the edge of the pool, eating a banana. Then Jan saw a sight that changed his cry of delight to a low, scarcely audible growl.

Swimming swiftly across the pool in the peculiar, zigzag manner of serpents was an immense anaconda. There was no mistaking its purpose. With its massive head swaying on its arched neck, and forked tongue darting from between its scaly lips, it swam straight for Chicma.

Jan shouted a warning, but too late.

For a moment the great head poised above the cringing ape. Then the jaws with their cruel, back-curved fangs, gaped wide and the serpent struck.

CHAPTER XIII

DR. BRACKEN'S CLUE

DR. BRACKEN KNEW, when he saw that Jan and Chicma had been carried off on a Venezuelan schooner, that his elaborate plans for revenge had been delayed. He would not admit that they had been defeated. He had always been a man of fixed purpose, and now his determination became so strong that nothing short of death itself could have stopped him.

Back in his office after his fruitless tramp through the swamp, he sat with his feet on his desk, smoking innumerable black stogies and scheming.

At first he thought of taking a steamer for Venezuela and checking up on the arrivals there. But his African trip and some unlucky stock ventures had reduced his fortune to a few thousand dollars, and his professional income had dwindled to scarcely more than a pittance a trip to South America would be expensive, and perhaps fruitless, as the schooner might have visited and left any one of a hundred other ports before he could reach it. Then, too, Chicma might have died at sea, for chimpanzees have delicate constitutions. In that case it would be almost impossible to trace Jan.

He could look up the names of all schooners sailing under the flag of Venezuela and write letters of inquiry to their masters, offering a reward. But this might implicate him in a kidnapping case.

He decided that his best plan would be to run blind advertisements regularly in the newspapers of Venezuela's chief seaports. So he inserted notices in all of them twice weekly for several months.

At the end of that time, when no answers had come, he wrote to the masters of all Venezuelan schooners, using an alias and living in Jacksonville for the purpose of getting his mail there under the assumed name. He received courteous replies from every ship's master to whom he had written, but not one could tell him what he sought to know.

In desperation Dr. Bracken resorted to his original plan, some nine months after Jan's escape. Selling his menagerie and what securities he had, he deposited the money in a Tampa bank, obtained letters of credit and left.

First he called at every United States port on the Gulf of Mexico. Then he obtained passports and called at every other port on the gulf, the Bay of Campeche, and the Caribbean Sea. Still unsuccessful, but unwilling to give up, he circled the entire continent of South America, spending some time in each port and returning via the Panama Canal.

Nearly three years after Jan's escape, he got back to Citrus Crossing with his meager fortune dissipated—only to find a letter there, postmarked "Cumana." With trembling, eager fingers, he opened it and read in Spanish:

DEAR SIR:
Today I bought a bottle of tequila, and the man who sold it to me wrapped it in an old newspaper. When I unwrapped it later I noticed your advertisement.

I am the ship's master who captured the ape you mention. With her was a wild boy with red hair. My ship, the Santa Margarita, was driven out of her course and sunk by a hurricane. The boy and ape, together with my first mate, a Haitian Negro, escaped into the jungle.

Having lost my fortune with my ship, and being compelled to earn my living as a day laborer, I have not had the means to pursue them. But I have heard rumors of their doings, and could easily locate them for you if supplied with the money to finance an expedition into the jungle. I should be delighted to undertake this for a reasonable compensation.

I am, sir, your most humble and obedient servant,

CAPTAIN FRANCESCO SANTOS.

Dr. Bracken thoughtfully stroked his iron-gray beard. Then he lit a black stogie and sat down, puffing fiercely. Fate, it seemed, had not only worked against him, but was now laughing at him. For she at last revealed the one person who could lead him to Jan—but after she had stripped him of the money needed for going after the boy.

The doctor was not a man to accept defeat, however, even from Fate. There would be a way to carry on; there must be a way.

Suddenly he slapped his thigh and laughed. An idea had occurred to him which appealed to his grim sense of humor. By a clever juggling of the facts he felt sure that Harry Trevor, Jan's father, could be made to pay all expenses for the expedition, including the doctor's own.

OVER IN the harbor of Tampa the palatial yacht *Georgia A.* rode idly at anchor, awaiting the whim of her master. This and Trevor's millions would be at his disposal, Dr. Bracken saw with satisfaction.

The Trevors were having tea on their spacious screened veranda when he drove up.

"Welcome home, Doc," said Harry Trevor, genially, rising and extending his hand as the doctor came in. "Have a pleasant trip"

Rather, replied the physician, as they shook hands. "As trips go, it wasn't half bad."

He released the young millionaire's hand and looked at Georgia Trevor with an involuntary catch of his breath. If anything, she grew more beautiful year by year in spite of her great sorrow. She was a trifle thinner, a little paler than she had been in that bygone time when his love had turned to hate. But her velvety skin was unmarred by wrinkles, and the shimmering copper of her hair was still untouched by the silversmith called

Time. Only in her big blue eyes, might one see the shadow of the tragedy that had all but deprived her of life itself—the tragedy which, though, she did not suspect, had been brought about by the man who was now smiling down at her, his white teeth gleaming against the dark background of his beard.

The doctor advanced and bowed low over her hand.

"I see you have been busy during my absence," he said.

"Busy? Doing what?"

"Growing more beautiful."

She laughed—a little silvery ripple that had an undertone of sadness.

"What'll it be, old man?" asked Trevor. "Tea, or something stronger? My bootlegger just brought me some excellent Scotch."

"Tea will do, thanks."

He took a seat at the table and watched Georgia as she gracefully poured the amber beverage. Trevor pushed lemons, sugar and cream before him.

The doctor helped himself to cream and sugar, and stirred his beverage thoughtfully for a moment. Finally he spoke.

"I don't want you to take it too seriously, yet," he said, "for it is possible that I am mistaken. However, I believe I have some great news for you two."

Georgia Trevor leaned forward eagerly.

"It's not about—it can't be about our baby!" she exclaimed.

"Yes."

The teacup dropped from her forgers, and the two men sprang to her support, as she seemed about to faint. But she steadied herself resolutely.

"I'm—I'm quite all right. Tell me!"

THE DOCTOR sat down once more, and Trevor collected the fragments of the shattered cup.

"You will remember that an ape of mine wandered away about three years ago," began the doctor. "A female chimpanzee.

She was a valuable animal and a favorite pet of mine, so I spared
no expense in my attempts to recapture her.

"I followed her into the swamp, but eventually lost the trail,
nor did I hear anything of her for several months afterward.
But one day while hunting I met an old 'cracker' who lived by
himself back in the swamps. He told a strange tale of having
seen the ape, in company with a red-headed youth about sixteen
years old, captured by the crew of a Venezuelan schooner. Both
were taken aboard the ship, which then sailed away.

"I doubted the tale at first, but as it was my sole remaining
clue, I decided to act upon it. I advertised in the leading Venezuelan newspapers without result. But today, upon my return,
a letter was waiting for me. Written in answer to my ad, it
confirms the strange story of the old cracker, who has since
died. How this boy and my chimpanzee came to be traveling
together is a mystery. Possibly the same person who kidnaped
your baby captured my ape. Perhaps, after becoming friends,
they escaped together. At any rate they were really captured
together, and together were shipwrecked on the coast of South
America. Listen to this."

He took the letter of Santos from his pocket, opened, and
read it.

Georgia Trevor turned to her husband, her eyes alight with
hope.

"It must be our boy, Harry!" she exclaimed. "I am sure it is.
Can't we go to South America at once and look for him? Oh,
I want him so!"

"We certainly can, dear," he said. "I'll send a wire to Tampa,
so the yacht will be provisioned and ready. Then we'll drive over
in the morning, get aboard, and be off." He turned to the doctor.
"You're coming with us, aren't you, Doc?"

The physician sighed.

"Like to," he responded, "but I'm afraid I can't. You see, I had
a little run of bad luck with stocks. I'm cleaned."

"Don't let that worry you, old man. I want to pay all expenses, you know. Insist on it. And we need you; not only because of your medical knowledge but because you are a seasoned traveler and jungle explorer. I'd like to have you take charge of the expedition on a salary—name it yourself—and all expenses paid. Just tell me how much you need at present, and I'll advance it now."

The details were soon settled. Money was cabled to Santos, and he was instructed to organize and take charge of a party for the expedition, and then to await the arrival of the yacht.

The next morning the *Georgia A.* steamed out of Tampa harbor, bound for South America.

CHAPTER XIV

THE HIDDEN VALLEY

JAN HESITATED FOR a moment when he saw the cruel jaws of the immense anaconda close on the shoulder of Chicma. Then, running lightly out to the end of the limb on which he stood, he dived for a point beside the great, thick coils that were slithering up out of the pool to encircle their victim.

Although it was a much higher dive than he had ever made, Jan struck the water cleanly and came up beside the serpent. Whipping out his *machete*, he hacked again and again at the writhing coils. The waters of the pool seethed with the struggles of man, ape and serpent.

Presently the anaconda released its hold on Chicma, who was, by this time, near the curtain of water dripping from above. She instantly scrambled through it, and Jan was left alone to fight it out with the huge reptile, which had now turned all its attention to him.

With jaws gaping and neck arched above the foaming water, it struck straight for his face. But although the dart of the serpent was incredibly swift, the counter-stroke of Jan was quicker. His *machete* flashed in, a shimmering arc, its keen edge half severing the reptile's enormous head from its body. Feebly, the snake attempted to strike again, but this time the *machete* completed its task, and the gaping head flew off to sink out of sight, while the scaly body continued to writhe and flounder aimlessly about in the water.

Jan's first concern was for Chicma, whom he had seen as she

crawled through the sheet of falling water. Plunging in after her, he found her huddled against the cliff beneath the falls, whimpering and licking her wounded shoulder.

"Come!" he barked in the chimpanzee language. "Let us go back to the hut."

"No. Sleepy One will get me."

"But he has gone to sleep forever."

"I will not go. He might wake up."

He coaxed, but to no avail.

Then he thought of the open valley at the other end of the cavern where he had met the hairy men. Perhaps he could persuade her to go that way. And anyhow, he wanted to explore the valley and to avenge himself on the hairy creatures who had attacked him. He would teach them and their kind to let him alone, as he had taught the Indians of the jungle.

He went back to the tree-hut, where he gathered an assortment of weapons: a bow and a quiverful of arrows, a blowgun with a supply of poisoned darts, and a spear. He also exchanged the *machete* he was carrying for one slightly larger and heavier.

Returning to where Chicma cowered beneath the waterfall, he said:

"Come. We leave this place."

She followed him obediently as he climbed the notches in the face of the cliff and entered the cave guarded by the hawk-faced and dog-faced statues. She was not afraid to go with him through the dark corridors of the cavern. But she balked when they reached the place where it was necessary to enter the water once more in order to get out into the sunlight. Twice she had been injured by monsters that had come up out of the water—an alligator and an anaconda—and she feared it.

After coaxing and arguing for some time to no avail, Jan decided to take his weapons through first, then come back after her. He made them into a bundle with the *curari*-tipped blowgun darts on the top, so the poison would not be washed from their points. Supporting the bundle, half in and half out of the water, with one hand he swam out into the sunlight. Making for the shore, he hid his bundle in a clump of reeds, then swam back into the cavern.

Chicma, seeing him return unhurt, finally decided to go back with him.

AS SOLICITOUS as a mother for her babe, Jan helped Chicma through the underground channel. She had cared for him in his years of helplessness, and now that she grew more dependent day by day, he felt that come what might he must care for her.

Emerging into the sunlight, they swam for the shore and climbed up the bank. Standing on the top, they shook themselves like two dogs.

Jan gathered up his weapons and they started off down the broken, weed-gown avenue. To the ape, the grotesque images which lined the approach to the temple ruins were only so many oddly shaped stones, but to the boy they were a source of wonder and curiosity. He eyed each one suspiciously as he came near it, fearful lest it should suddenly come to life and attack them. He also kept a sharp lookout for his former enemies, the hairy men.

On reaching the portal of the ruined temple, they advanced cautiously, Jan keeping his weapons in readiness in case some unseen enemy should leap out from behind a pillar or fallen rock fragment.

A large part of the roof had caved in, but many sections were still intact. The walls were decorated with brightly colored murals, and much statuary stood about on pedestals and in niches. The floor was of smooth, well-matched tiles laid in geometric designs. All of these things appealed tremendously to Jan's inherent artistic and aesthetic nature, so that he proceeded slowly in order to gaze his fill at the new wonders constantly appearing before him.

The building consisted of a central auditorium, around which were many corridors and anterooms. At one end of the great hall; on a semicircular platform, stood a colossal image of a man with a thin, sickle-like beard curving outward from the point of his chin. On the head was a tall crown, ornamented on each side with a curling plume and a twisted horn, and in front with a smooth, golden disk. One huge hand held a three-lashed whip, and the other a short-handled crook.

Passing on through the ruins of the building Jan and Chicma emerged in the remains of what had once been a large and magnificent garden, circled by a high stone wall. Despite the fact that it was overgrown with weeds and creepers, there remained many flowers, shrubs and trees. In the center an ornate fountain of marble and carnelian splashed musically.

At the far end of the garden was a small, vine-covered bower. Jan wandered toward this, admiring several small statuettes which stood along the pathway, while Chicma made straight for an orange tree near the wall.

He had passed the fountain only a little way when he saw something that caused him to stiffen in his tracks, then silently dart behind a clump of shrubbery. A thing inside the bower had moved; an immense thing with striped sides and back, and a huge, cat-like head.

LOADING HIS blow-gun with a poisoned dart, Jan waited tensely. The great shaggy head slowly emerged into the pathway, followed by a striped body as large as that of a burro. With tasseled ears laid back and eight-inch tusks gleaming, its appearance was terror-striking.

Jan recognized the creature instantly from a picture he had seen in one of Ramona's books. It was a saber-toothed tiger, and Ramona had told him it belonged to a past age, that there were no longer any such creatures on earth. Apparently she had been misinformed.

The primeval giant cat had evidently been awakened from its nap by the sound of their entrance into its retreat, and resented it. Noting the direction of its baleful gaze, Jan saw that it was watching Chicma as she sat on one of the lower branches of the orange tree, greedily devouring the fragrant fruit.

Jan put his blow-gun to his lips and sped a tiny dart at the monster. The slender missile embedded itself in the great striped shoulder, and clung. The creature shook itself; dislodging it. Evidently the small projectile had not caused this big cat any more inconvenience or pain than the sting of an insect.

Knowing the usual effect of the *curari* poison with which he had tipped the dart, Jan waited, expecting to see the creature sink down dead in its tracks. But instead, it charged straight for the tree in which Chicma was feeding, uttering a roar louder and more terrible than any Jan had ever heard.

As the beast charged, Jan sent a second dart into its side. He shot a third into its heaving flank as it leaped for the lower branches of the orange tree.

Chicma had taken one look at the charging carnivore and scampered for the topmost branches of the tree, but when she saw it leaping up toward her she swung over the top of the high wall and dropped out of sight on the other side.

The poison from the first dart had evidently not been enough to paralyze the motor nerves of the huge beast. But the triple dose began to take effect as it caught the lower branches of the tree. It clung to them for a moment, snarling and roaring, then fell to the ground on its back.

Jan knew that no member of the cat tribe would fall on its back from that height unless it was very near death, so he waited. After thrashing about for some time in the undergrowth, the mighty killer finally lay still.

Before approaching it, Jan fired an arrow into the carcass. As no movement followed, he was convinced that the monster was sleeping its last long sleep, and advanced to examine it. For some time he looked the beast over, marveling at its long, sickle-shaped claws, its bulging muscles, and its immense saber-like tusks. What a fearful antagonist it would make! Jan had fought the jaguar and the puma, *machete* against teeth and claws, and won, but he felt very dubious indeed about the outcome of such a duel with one of these monsters.

However, it had gone to sleep now, never to waken. He must reassure Chicma. He called to her, but there was no reply. He called again at the top of his voice. Still no answer.

Alarmed, he scrambled up the orange tree and onto the top of the wall. He was looking out over a vast, rolling plain—a savanna of tall, waving grass, dotted here and there with clumps of trees. Meeting at the point where the river went underground and traveling as far as he could see to the right and left, until lost in the blue haze, was an unbroken line of tall cliffs, encircling the valley through which the river meandered. Beyond the plain before him was a dense forest, Chicma's trail of trampled grass led that way; she had set out for the jungles of this great closed valley.

After caching his blow-gun darts and spear in one of the anterooms of the temple in order to lighten his burden, Jan hurried after the chimpanzee, following the plainly marked trail with ease through the tall, rustling grass.

This grass, with its rough cutting edges, reminded Jan of the sawgrass he had encountered in the Everglades. It brought hateful memories of Dr. Bracken, and the life he had lived as a prisoner in the menagerie.

He had thought he would easily catch up with the aged Chicma in a few minutes, but before he had gone far he knew that her great fright at the saber-toothed tiger had caused her to run much faster than usual. At last he caught sight of her, just passing over the brow of a low hill ahead.

THEN HE saw something that checked the shout on his lips and brought him to an abrupt halt—a row of hideous monsters, with sharp horns on the tips of their noses and just above their eyes, were galloping over the hill. Their shoulders were protected by great bony ruffs, and behind these, mounted on their backs, sat men clad in shiny yellow armor and carrying long lances.

Knights—mounted on triceratops! Jan recognized both from pictures he had seen in Ramona's books. But she had said that both belonged to the past, that such things were no more.

With a shriek of fear, Chicma turned and attempted to flee, but in a twinkling she was surrounded, and a half dozen of the armored men had alighted and were advancing toward her.

Jan's first impulse at sight of that formidable host was to run. But when he saw Chicma surrounded, his loyalty held him. Fitting an arrow to his bowstring, he launched it at the man who stood nearest to the cowering chimpanzee. To his surprise, the six-foot shaft rebounded harmlessly from the glistening yellow cuirass. He released a second, and this glanced off the metal helmet, narrowly missing Chicma.

But the first arrow had revealed his presence to the enemy. Wild shouts of the armored men mingled with the hoarse bellows and thundering hoof beats of their fearsome mounts as they charged. In a trice he was surrounded by a circle that bristled with triple-horned heads and glittering lance points.

Jan dropped his bow, whipped out his heavy *machete,* and stood at bay. Several of his assailants dismounted and came toward him carrying long, two-edged swords in their hands. A moment more and he would have been cut to ribbons, had not there come a sharp command from one of the men who had remained mounted. At this, the advancing warriors sheathed their weapons and leaped in, clutching him with their mailed hands.

Despite his valiant resistance, his *machete* was soon wrested from him, his wrists were bound together behind his back, and he was flung into a saddle in front of one of the riders.

As the cavalcade moved away, Jan saw with relief that Chicma, too, was a prisoner, and not slain as he had feared.

Although the great beasts which carried the mailed warriors were ponderous and clumsy-looking, they traveled across the grassy plain at a considerable speed. It was not long before they reached the forest which Jan had seen from the wall of the ruins. It was much like his jungle of the outside world, though many of the plants were new and strange to him. Here shrub, tree and vine intermingled in such a thick and impenetrable tangle that/the riders were forced to pass, single file, along a narrow tunnel which had evidently been cut for the purpose through the thickly interwoven vegetation.

A MOMENT later there flashed through Jan's nimble mind a plan for making his escape. They had entered one of the thickest and darkest parts of the jungle when he suddenly pivoted in the saddle, catching the man who rode behind him with his elbow, just below the armpit, and hurled him off his mount to the right. Almost at the same instant, he threw himself into the thicket at his left.

Because his hands were bound behind him, Jan fell on his face in the undergrowth. But he quickly scrambled to his feet and dashed away. The shouts of men, the clank of armor and the crashing of jungle growths apprised him of pursuit, and he hurried breathlessly onward.

Although the swift mounts and heavy armor of the warriors had been to their advantage for capturing Jan in the open, they were a hindrance in the jungle. Soon they fell so far behind that the sounds of pursuit came but faintly to the fugitive's ears. But he did not slacken his pace.

The jungle came to an end with unexpected abruptness, and Jan found himself on the margin of a small stream thickly dotted with water lilies. Just in front of him a black-robed figure—a white man—stood in the stern of a black boat, built and carved to resemble a huge alligator with head and tail up-curved from the water. The man in the black robe, a thickset, ruddy-faced, bullet-headed fellow with a shaved poll, held a long, stout pole with which he was evidently about to push off from shore. But as soon as he saw Jan, the robed man quickly shifted his hold and swung the pole bludgeon-like for his head. Jan dodged, and turned to reenter the shelter of the jungle.

But at that moment his feet slipped on the muddy bank, and

he fell, face downward. The boatman's long staff, which he had avoided the first time, swung again as he tried to scramble to his feet. This time it struck him squarely on the right temple, and brought oblivion.

CHAPTER XV

THE BLACK PRISON

WHEN JAN RECOVERED consciousness once more he was lying in the bottom of the boat, which the black-robed man was poling up the narrow stream. He tried to move, and found that not only his wrists, but his ankles also, were bound. Piled in the boat around him were many baskets of lotus plants which his captor had gathered.

At first they passed only the moss-draped, liana-laced border of the jungle, but they presently arrived at a place where a high wall of black marble fronted the stream. The prow of the boat grounded at the base of a flight of steps which led up from the water's edge to a massive gate that barred a great arched gateway. At each side of this stood a guard in black armor, holding a long pike and wearing a sword and dagger.

The man in the boat shouted, and the gate swung back. A dozen black-robed figures came through it and down the steps. Some of them dragged the prow of the boat higher, while others took out the baskets of lotus plants. Many exclaimed in apparent surprise as they saw Jan lying bound in the bottom of the boat, but none offered to touch him.

When the cargo of plants had been removed, Jan's captor looped a rope around his neck. Then he drew a knife from his girdle and cut the rope that bound his ankles, signing for him to rise.

Jan stood up, and his head swam dizzily, for it was still rocking from the blow he had received. But his captor, with a

93

hoarse command which he could not comprehend, stepped out
of the boat and tugged at the rope circling his neck—an un-
spoken order which the captive understood very well—and
which he had to obey.

After following his conductor up the steps, Jan was led
through an immense garden of well-kept flowers, shrubs and
trees. It was decorated with statuary depicting some figures of
rare beauty and others of surpassing ugliness. And dotted here
and there were pools and fountains. In some of these pools were
sacred lotuses, budding and in full bloom; in others, Jan saw
the black-robes setting out the plants which had just been taken
from the nearby stream.

Having crossed the garden, they entered a doorway where
two more black-armored pikemen stood guard in an immense
building of black marble. Then they followed for some distance
a long corridor, the floor of which was of black and silver tiles,
and the walls of which were decorated with brightly colored
murals. Many doorways opened into this corridor, but Jan's
captor did not pause until he reached a great arched opening
at its very end.

Here he was halted by two guards, each of whom, in addition
to his sword and dagger, carried an immense broad-ax. After
exchanging a few words with Jan's captor, they permitted him
to pass into a large central room, the domed ceiling of which
resembled the sky on a starlit, moonless night. Conspicuous
among the sparkling constellations was—though Jan, of course
did not know what it was—a magnified representation of the
planet Saturn, showing globe and rings as they would look
through a telescope.

Jan stared in wonder and amazement at this vivid and exag-
gerated representation of the nighttime sky. Then his attention
was attracted by a group of black-robed figures standing on the
other side of the room at the right and left of a great, black
throne.

His captor jerked him roughly forward, nearly choking him,
and advancing obsequiously, knelt before the black throne.

SEATED ON the throne was a man whose emaciated features were of chalky paleness—a white skin stretched over a nearly fleshless skull. On his head was a shimmering silver helmet, the crest of which was fashioned to represent the arched head and neck of an alligator. It sparkled with many jewels, dominated by an immense emerald that flashed above the center of his forehead.

His lank body was encased, also, in silver armor, and over his shoulders was thrown a long, black cape, broidered and bordered with silver and jewels. Depending from about his neck by a slender chain was a ball of silver, circled with many concentric disks of the same metal—an emblem of the planet, Saturn.

As he stared down at Jan, his ghastly features were immobile, inscrutable. Only his sunken eyes, which glowed with the greenish light that characterizes the orbs of night-prowling beasts showed any signs of animation. And their gaze was baleful—menacing.

After looking at Jan for a moment, he addressed a few words to his captor. The latter replied at some length. When he had finished, the man on the throne made a sign with his right hand. As he did so, the youth noticed that in his palm was tattooed a blue flower like that in the paten of Ramona, a copy of which was in Jan's own palm.

In response to the gesture, a fat, black-robed, shaved-headed fellow with heavy pink jowls came and bowed before the throne, extending a metal box with the lid thrown back. From this box the man on the throne selected a jeweled bracelet, which he tossed to Jan's still kneeling captor. Then he clapped his hands, whereupon two armored guards clanked into the room from a door at the side of the dais.

At a word of command from the man on the throne, each of them seized Jan by an arm, and together they marched him away. After they had gone down a narrow and tortuous corridor for a long way, they came out into a sunlit courtyard paved with black granite. Crossing this, they arrived before a massive gate, guarded by four armored pikemen and four ax-men.

One of the pikemen drew back a heavy bar, and the gate swung open. After removing the rope from around Jan's neck and cutting his bonds with a dagger, his two conductors pushed him through. Bewildered, he looked about him as the gate closed behind him.

He stood in a long, rectangular pen surrounded by twenty-foot walls built of large granite blocks, smooth-faced and so carefully fitted together that it was barely possible to see where they joined.

In the pen were several hundred men—not white like his captors, yet lighter in color than the Indians he had encountered in the jungle. Their skin seemed to vary from light tan to yellow. Some of them closely resembled Indians except for their lighter skins, but the eyes of most of them slanted more, and their cheek bones were more pronounced. All wore leather breech clouts and sandals of twisted grass, and some had gaudily colored blankets thrown over their shoulders.

They were squatting on the ground or standing around in little groups, conversing. But as soon as Jan entered he became the target for their glances, and evidently the chief subject of their conversation. Many crowded around him, chattering excitedly, and staring as if he were some strange beast on exhibition. The ring drew closer.

Jan snarled menacingly. He disliked Indians, for with a single exception they had always proved hostile to him; always sought his life. These men reminded him of Indians. But they gave way before him as he strode forward, stiffly erect and alert for attack, toward the gate at the opposite end of the inclosure. Perhaps they were awed by the fire that flashed from his steel-gray eyes. Or they may have been impressed by the powerful muscles that rippled beneath his smooth skin.

Having crossed the inclosure without being touched, Jan sat down in the shadow of the gate. Although many slanting eyes still stared at him, no one had followed. He considered plans for escape. He could not scale the twenty-foot walls unaided.

Furthermore, at intervals of thirty feet around the rim were small sentry towers, each of which held two archers. Great stealth would be required, even on the darkest night, to avoid these alert watchers and escape with a whole skin.

CHAPTER XVI

THE DAY OF PAYMENT

ABRUPTLY THE GATE behind Jan swung open. He sprang
to his feet as four black-armored men entered, marching abreast,
carrying long swords in their hands. Behind them came a file
of slant-eyed, yellow-skinned slaves, naked save for breech
clouts and sandals. Each slave bore an immense tray on his
head, and Jan saw that some were heaped high with fruits, some
with chunks of cooked meat, and some with golden-brown
cakes. Following these slaves were others who bore large earth-
enware jars on their heads, and around whose waists cups
hanging from wire hooks jingled musically.

As the gate closed behind them, the slaves carrying the trays
knelt in a row, still holding them on their heads. Those who
carried the jars also knelt, and set them on the ground. The
occupants of the inclosure, meanwhile, hurried to form a long
line, jostling and crowding each other for the places nearest the
front. Then, at a shout from one of the swordsmen, they filed
past the row of kneeling slaves, where each was supplied with
a piece of meat, a cake, some fruit, and a cupful of brown beverage which was dipped from the jars, and which Jan afterward
learned was called *chocolatl*. The four swordsmen stood by, to
see that no one got more than his share.

Jan was hungry, having eaten nothing since entering the
valley. He went to one of the meat trays and was about to help
himself when a swordsman shouted something to him which
he could not understand, and ran between him and the tray,

brandishing his weapon. Under the menace of the keen blade, Jan backed away, the guard following him chattering and gesticulating.

He was made to understand that he must take his place in the line, at the very end. So carefully had the supply of rations been computed that when Jan finally reached them, but one portion of each thing was left. With his meat, cake and fruit held in the curve of his left arm before him, and his cup of *chocolatl* in his right hand, he made his way through the jostling crowd. The slaves and swordsmen withdrew, and he heard the gate slam shut after them.

Suddenly a brown hand reached over his shoulder from behind and snatched his meat. With a low growl of rage, Jan whirled to confront the pilferer. But there were no less than a half dozen men behind him, each of whom might have been guilty. Each wore an innocent expression, and none seemed to have more than one piece of meat.

Enraged and disappointed at losing his favorite food, but unable to tell who snatched it, he turned away to seek a spot where he might eat the remainder of his rations undisturbed. Then a youth of about his own age stepped in front of him with a friendly smile, and tearing his own piece of meat in two, offered him half.

Jan was nonplussed. The anger surging within him made him feel like flying at any one who crossed his path. But his wrath dissolved before that disarming smile and unselfish offer. He accepted the meat, and the two lads sat down side by side to eat, neither knowing that this was to be the beginning of a friendship that would be strong and lasting.

They conversed by signs at first, but Jan soon made his companion understand that he wished to know the names of things, by pointing to or touching them and looking at him questioningly. As he was quick to learn and had an excellent memory, it was not long before he was combining verbs and adjectives with his nouns, and forming short sentences in this new language.

WEEKS PASSED, and though many prisoners were taken away and new ones brought in, Jan and his companion remained. During this time, Jan learned the language of the yellow people, and also a considerable portion of that of their white captors, which his friend taught him.

The yellow-skinned youth's name was Koh Kan, Koh being his given name and Kan both his family name and title. Tattooed in the palm of his right hand was a picture of a feathered serpent, done in red. This, he told Jan, was a picture of Kan, the mighty serpent, earthly representative of the Fair God, Quetzalcoatl, whose abode was in the sun, but who was expected to return some day to earth. Koh's father, he said, was hereditary ruler of his race and High Priest of Kan, so he was Prince Koh of the House of Kan. Jan had only a hazy idea of the position of a prince, but he had noticed the great respect shown this one by the yellow prisoners, and judged that it must be quite important.

Koh said his people lived in a great city called Temukan, which was a long, dangerous journey away, beyond an immense, muddy pit in which roved terrible and gigantic monsters. They were always at war with the white people, he said, whose chief city was called Satmu, and who worshiped a number of gods. His people, he said, had but one sect and worshiped Quetzalcoatl in the person of Kan, the great feathered serpent, who was propitiated with human sacrifice—prisoners of war and convicted criminals.

The white people, he said, were divided into four sects who worshiped two gods Re and Asar; a goddess, Aset; and a demon, Set—whose earthly representative was Sebek, a very terrible living water monster. They also did homage to three minor divinities.

The Sect of Re, he said, wore gold-plated armor, or clothing of a golden yellow color—such as had first captured Jan. That of Asar wore white, and that of Aset light blue. But the Sect of Set wore black.

"You and I," he told Jan, "have been captured by the people of Set."

"For what purpose?" asked Jan.

"Each day," said Koh, "you have noticed that two men are taken away, never to return?"

"Yes, I have noticed that," replied Jan.

"They are fed to the monster, Sebek," said Koh. "Some day we, too, shall be fed to him, as will every man in this place."

"What is he like?" Jan wanted to know.

"There are said to be monsters like him in the great pit of mud which lies near the center of the valley, but nowhere else," Koh told him. "His head and long jaws are like those of an alligator, but many times bigger. His body is very long, and his feet are like the fins of a fish. Here, I will show you."

With the tip of his finger he sketched a picture of the creature he had described. Then arising, he continued: "He is said to be this long," and stepped off twenty paces, or about fifty feet.

"But if there are other creatures like this," said Jan, "why is it that they feed men to this one only?"

"He is selected from among the others by the High Priest," Koh replied, "who makes certain tests to ascertain whether or not the soul of Set has descended into him. This only happens about once in five generations, as the beasts are very long-lived, and a new one is selected from the pit only when an old one dies."

At every opportunity Jan made inquiries about Chicma, but he learned nothing until one day when a prisoner who had formerly been a slave of the golden Sect of Re told him he had seen her, and that she was kept as an object of great curiosity in the royal palace of Satmu, having been presented to the empress by the captain of a band of huntsmen who had captured her.

A few days after that, as Jan and Koh sat talking, four guards walked up to where they sat.

"It is the summons!" whispered Koh. "We are to be fed to Sebek! Farewell, friend Jan. I hope that we may meet and be friends in the next world."

The two lads embraced, but were quickly torn apart by the guards, who hustled them away.

CHAPTER XVII

A WARM TRAIL

ON ONE OF the long wooden docks that projected over the river in front of the Suarez hacienda, Don Fernando and Doña Isabella, as well as a score of their Indian servants, stood gazing intently downstream. Today Ramona was expected home from her first year of school in the United States. A servant had just come dashing up to the house to announce that the boats were coming.

After gazing for a brief interval, Don Fernando removed his slim cigar from between his lips and said to his wife:

"The *mozo* was wrong. Those are not our canoes."

"But they must be," insisted Doña Isabella. "Who else would be coming this way with so many boats?"

The don shrugged.

"Explorers, perhaps, or a party of hunters. We'll soon see."

There were six canoes in all, most of them smaller than the six sent out by Don Fernando in charge of Felipe Fuez, his foreman, with orders to meet and bring Ramona and her governess.

As the first canoe drew near to the dock, the don carefully scanned the faces of its occupants. Besides the four Indian paddlers it contained two white men—one a swarthy Venezuelan with a small, pointed mustache, the other a lean, bearded man wearing a pith helmet and khaki, who might be an American or an Englishman. In the second boat rode two more people with pith helmets and khaki clothing. One was a broad-shouldered, clean-shaven, athletic-looking fellow who appeared to be in his middle thirties; the other was a woman, somewhat younger and quite comely, whose curls glinted auburn in the reflected sunbeams that danced up from the river. The other four boats contained Indian paddlers and luggage.

The first canoe came up beside the dock. Its gunwale was seized by willing hands, steadied.

The don and doña were smiling and gracious now, masking their disappointment at not seeing Ramona, that they might welcome the strangers with fitting cordiality.

When the first two stood on the dock the bearded man took the initiative.

"I am Dr. Bracken, Don Fernando," he said in Spanish.

"I am honored, *señor*," replied the don. "Doña Isabella, may I present Dr. Bracken?"

"An honor and a pleasure," murmured the doctor, when the doña had acknowledged the introduction. "May I present Captain Santos?

"My other companions speak very little Spanish," he added then. "Permit me to translate for you."

"Hardly necessary," smiled the don. "I'm a Harvard man, and the doña attended Lake Forest University. We first met in the States at a football game."

"Splendid!" replied the doctor. "Then the introductions will be in English."

And so they were. Doña Isabella and Mrs. Trevor soon found much in common, due to the former's residence in the Stales.

SUDDENLY THERE came a cry from an Indian at the end of the dock.

"More canoes coming!"

Don Fernando looked down the river. Two had rounded the bend. A third was just nosing into sight.

"*Viva!*" he cried. "Our boats!"

"It's our daughter, Ramona," explained Dana Isabella.

*Jan swung himself up on
the ichthyosaur's scaly neck,*

The first canoe came on swiftly, outdistancing the others. It glided toward the pier, propelled by the don's best paddlers, and steered by Ruiz himself, a big fellow with a snow-white mustache and goatee. He deftly guided it to the dock amid shouts of welcome:

As many willing hands steadied the boat, Ramona stood up, leaped lightly out, ran into the arms of Doña Isabella, kissed and hugged Don Fernando. There were tears of joy in the eyes of all three. The don held her away from him, admiring her proudly.

"How you have grown, my little one! And how stunning you look in those 'flapper' clothes!"

Many other pairs of eyes also admired the trim little figure, the lustrous dark eyes and hair, and the skin of milk and roses. The usually half-closed orbs of Captain Santos opened wide and he gasped involuntarily. As his eyes drank in Ramona's youthful loveliness, passion flamed suddenly in his breast, was reflected in the flush that mounted to his throbbing temples:

Suddenly self-conscious and fearful lest he had been noticed, he tore his eyes away and fumbled for a cigarette. Not until he had lighted it did he cast a furtive glance around him. No one, it seemed, had observed him. With a sigh of relief, he exhaled a cloud of blue smoke.

But there was one who had seen, and understood fully. Dr. Bracken, outwardly unmoved, was inwardly gloating. For many days he had been looking for a rope with which to bind Santos to his cause. Now it was revealed to him as plainly as if the captain had spoken his thoughts aloud.

Fussing like a brooding hen, the short and rotund duenna, Señora Soledade, was on the dock now.

Doña Isabella was introducing Ramona and Georgia Trevor. The girl started perceptibly as she clasped the hand of the auburn-haired woman and for the first time had a good look at her features.

"What as wrong?" asked the older woman.

"It's—it's nothing at, all. You look wonderful. You remind me strangely of someone else."

Don Fernando gave some crisp orders about the luggage. The Indians scrambled to obey, and the party moved toward the house.

According to Don Fernando's code, it would have been very bad taste to ask the purpose of his guests' expedition.

The subject did not come up until all had gathered for dinner.

"I'm curious to know," said Georgia Trevor to Ramona, "about this person who so greatly resembles me."

"His name is Jan," replied Ramona, "and he is only a little older than I. He once rescued me from a puma."

The effect of this statement on the four guests was electric. The eyes of Santos narrowed slightly. Dr. Bracken retained perfect control of his features, but he could not prevent the sudden pallor that spread over them at the mention of Jan's name. Harry Trevor's face showed his intense interest: that of his wife, sudden hope.

"Slightly older than you—resembling me!" she cried. "Harry, it must be our boy! He would be nineteen now. Tell me more about him, my dear—tell me all about him!"

With flashing eyes, Ramona related the story of her rescue. Her description of Jan was so favorable that her hero worship was obvious to all. She said nothing about her frequent meetings with him, although she hoped to resume them. Don Fernando had given his opinion of Jan quite plainly.

"*Por Dios!*" exclaimed the captain. That ees him, all right! Ees wan dangerous hombre, too, I tal' you. Me, I rather meet the hongry puma, any time."

"He's dangerous only to those who would harm him," flashed Ramona. "I am not afraid to meet him."

"I feel," interposed Harry Trevor, "that we owe our host and hostess an explanation. If you don't mind, my dear," with a look at his wife "I'll begin at the beginning and tell them why we have come into the South American jungles."

She nodded assent, and while all listened in rapt attention, and with varying emotions, he related the entire tale. The don and doña were sympathetic, eager to help. Ramona hoped that these people, whom she had begun to like very much, would really prove to be Jan's parents.

After dinner coffee, liqueurs and cigars were served on the terrace that overlooked the patio, and quite early everyone retired.

THE ROOMS of Dr. Bracken and the captain were opposite each other. As they walked down the hall together, the doctor invited Santos in for a chat. Santos sat down and lit a cigarette while the doctor softly closed the door. After listening for a moment, he returned and flung himself into a chair.

"It's about time, captain," the doctor said evenly, "that you and I came to a complete understanding. I'm not going to beat around the bush. You want to make money, don't you?"

"*Sí.*"

"And today you saw something which you want even more than money."

"I don't gat you."

"Yes you do. I wasn't blind today, Santos, when we stood on the pier as a certain party arrived. Now, suppose I am willing to help you realize your desire. Would you be willing to help me realize a certain wish of my own? To work with me and keep your mouth shut?"

"*Sí, señor.* I work to beat hal' and keep the mouth shut tight."

"Fine! Now what do you suppose would happen if you were to go to Don Fernando and propose marriage with his young daughter?"

"Planty!"

"Yes. He'd kick you out of the house. Now suppose you were to approach the daughter and suggest that she elope with you?"

The captain shrugged.

"Who knows what a woman will do, *señor?*"

"You know and I know that she is not likely to consider the plea of a stranger twice her age when she is in love with a handsome youth.

"So I theenk you right. She's craz' about that keed, for sure."

"Now where do you come in? What are your plans? You probably intend to steal that child, run away with her at the first opportunity. You will try to force marriage upon her—break down her will. If you succeed you will be the husband of the heiress to the Suarez millions. Sooner or later her people would take her back, and you with her. Suppose, on the other hand, that she would not marry you under any consideration. You could demand, and probably get a princely ransom. Failing in this, you would still have the girl—and to you, she herself would be worth the ransom of a grandee. Am I right?"

"If so, what then?"

"Simply this: I want to find Jan at once and keep him away from this house until it fits certain plans that I have to bring him here. I don't want his parents or their friends to hear of his capture. If you are willing to help me and say nothing, I'll be glad to do the same for you. Well, what do you say?"

"I say, O.K. *amigo.* I'm weeth you till the cow goes home."

CHAPTER XVIII

A DEATH HOLIDAY

A GREAT CROWD filled the open-air Temple of Sebek, a circular amphitheater near the great black Temple of Set. Word had gone forth that two unusual sacrifices would go into the capacious maw of the great fish-reptile Sebek this day—a prince of the House of Kan, and a strange white savage.

Not only were many black-robed priests present, and black-armored warriors, but there were also nobles of the order of Set, with their black cloaks, in special seats reserved for them, In other sections were tradesmen, artisans, artists, scribes, musicians and laborers. Although their costumes varied greatly in pattern and richness, all wore black, which identified them as the followers of Set. No women or children were present.

On a raised platform of black marble stood Samsu, High Priest of Set and cousin of the Emperor Mena, in his sacrificial robes and ornaments. His pasty, skull-like countenance turned slowly from side to side, and his small snaky eyes sparkled with satisfaction as he noted how vast an audience had gathered to view this special sacrifice.

The feeding of Sebek was a daily rite at the sun's zenith, and was therefore so common that when ordinary prisoners were sacrificed no one attended except those priests and warriors whose presence was commanded. But it was not often that Sebek feasted on royalty, and the white savage was a distinct novelty.

The High Priest looked down at the monster, a gigantic

ichthyosaur, swimming back and forth in the deep pool, the surface of which was about ten feet below the bottom tier of seats. Sebek was always hungry, and unusually active whenever his feeding time drew near. The jewel-studded gold rings in his ears and nostrils clattered as he reared his monstrous head from the water; snorting and snapping his jaws, which bristled with sharp teeth and were large enough to take in a grown man at a single gulp.

Then Samsu looked over at the two youths who stood on a slab of black stone opposite him, that hung out over the pool. The white man, whose sole garment was a ragged piece of jaguar skin, was gazing down into the pool, watching the movements of the monster with apparent interest, but with no signs of fear. The yellow prince, who wore the royal red of the House of Kan, stood stiffly erect, his gaze haughty, fearless. Behind them was a closed door, fitted snugly flush with the edges of the smooth wall. At a signal from the High Priest, the polished slab on which they stood would tilt straight downward.

Jan looked up from his examination of the creature in the pool.

"A mighty monster, this Sebek," he said to Koh.

"And terrible," replied Koh, speaking softly so he would not be overheard. "Think of the number of people that slimy monster has eaten in its long lifetime! And we, too, now go to our destiny by way of that filthy maw. See how the Black Ones have gathered, like buzzards around the dead! It will soon be over, friend Jan. Samsu has taken the mallet, and is squinting at the sun. At the third stroke of the gong, we drop."

"Then listen to me, and act quickly," replied Jan. "The pool has an inlet and an outlet. The inlet is at our right, the outlet at our left. Look down at the outlet now. Fix its position in your mind. Don't wait for the third stroke of the gong. Dive as soon as you hear the first, straight toward that outlet. Remain under water and swim into it. The monster has made the pool turbid with its movements, so you will not be seen. When you are deep in the outlet so no one can see you, rise and turn on your back. Thus you may breathe in the narrow air space at the top and swim out to freedom. The monster is too large to follow you through the opening."

"But what of you?" questioned Koh. "Will you come with me?"

"Later," replied Jan.

"I refuse to go if you intend to sacrifice yourself to save me," said Koh.

"Do as I say!" insisted Jan. "It is the only hope for both of us. Get ready. The High Priest is about to strike."

SAMSU STRUCK the great gong that hung behind him. It responded with a booming, metallic note. To the surprise of all present, the bodies of the two youths flashed outward from the slab in a simultaneous, graceful dive. Before the second note had boomed forth, both were under water.

As Jan and Koh had dived in opposite directions, the monster was confused for a moment, not knowing which way to turn. Koh, in accordance with his instructions, swam straight for the outlet, remaining beneath the surface. But Jan, who had dived beneath the monster's belly, came up beside it, and to the intense amazement of the spectators, grasped one of the bejeweled rings that hung from the rim of Sebek's short ear. Then he swung himself up on its scaly back, just behind the head.

This unexpected trick was greeted with cries of astonishment from the spectators, and with frantic efforts on the part of the ichthyosaur to unseat its rider. But as it thrashed about, Jan gripped the immense neck with his thighs and clung to an earring with each hand.

The spectators were getting far more entertainment than they had expected.

Presently the monster dived. In a few moments it emerged riderless, with blood streaming from its eye sockets, dyeing the water a pale crimson. As the multitude cried out in horror at this sacrilege, it began swimming blindly in a circle. Of the two intended victims they could see no trace.

As soon as the great fish-lizard had plunged beneath the water with Jan, he had put into effect the plan which had come to him when he saw its great resemblance to an alligator. He had plunged his fingers into its eyes.

Then he kicked himself away from the great bulk and swam toward the south wall. Following this, he explored with his hands until he came to the mouth of the outlet. Into this he plunged. After a few swift strokes, he rose to the surface, turned on his back, and drew great sobbing breaths of air into his aching lungs.

He swam in total darkness for a long time, despite the fact that the swift current and his own efforts were carrying him rapidly forward. It was with great relief that he finally saw a faint light ahead. Increasing his efforts, Jan shot out of the culvert into the sluggish current of a broad river. Quickly turning over, he gained the bank with half a dozen stout strokes and, seizing an overhanging root, drew himself up, dripping and triumphant.

IN FRONT of him the bushes parted and Koh emerged, his finger to his lips. Faintly Jan heard the sound of voices, the clank of armor and weapons, and the thunderous tread of great beasts, mingled with their occasional hoarse bellowings. Together, the two fugitives crouched in the shelter of the bushes.

"A hunting party of the Golden Ones," whispered Koh. "They will soon pass."

They crouched there breathlessly while the sounds grew alarmingly louder. Presently, however, they began to recede, and were lost in the distance.

"They've gone," said Jan. "And now, friend Koh, our paths lie in different directions. You will want to get back to Temukan as soon as possible. I go to Satmu to rescue Chicma."

"Come to Temukan with me, my friend," pleaded Koh. "You can't hope to rescue Chicma from the very palace of the

Emperor. First there is the river to cross. The bridges are guarded night and day. You have no boat, and if you swim there are man-eating monsters in the stream which can't be eluded so easily as the clumsy Sebek.

"Even if you succeed in reaching the island, so well guarded are the city walls and the palace itself that you can't hope to penetrate both without being either killed or captured. And you might as well be killed outright as captured, because if they take you alive, your death will only be a matter of a few days. Besides, if Samsu learns of your capture, he is sure to demand you from his imperial cousin, Mena, so he may torture and slay you as a punishment for what you have done today. He would probably give half his wealth to have you in his power right now.

"But even if you are captured and Samsu does not hear of it, you can't expect a much kinder fate from the Emperor. He will have you entered in the games, where human prisoners are forced to fight each other or huge and terrible beasts, some of which have been brought in from that place of horrors, the pit of mud. Not one prisoner in a hundred escapes the games alive. Come with me to the city of my father, the city which I will some day rule. Wealth, power, lands, slaves—everything you could wish shall be yours."

"I would like to go with you, my comrade," replied Jan. "But my duty calls me to Satmu, and that is where I am going."

"Well, then," said Koh. "I'll go with you."

"To meet all those dangers for a cause that does not concern your' I can't permit it!"

"I owe you my life," replied Koh. "Surely you will allow me to pay part of the debt! Besides, I will enjoy the adventure. With my knowledge of the country and people you will have a much better chance for success, too."

"As you will," said Jan, reluctantly.

"Now," said Koh, "if we swim the river the chances are ten to one that we will not get across alive. If we should elude the monsters that live in it, we would be seen and captured by boatmen. But if we search along the bank we are very likely to find a boat which we can steal under cover of darkness, and which will take us across in safety. While we are looking for the boat we may find something to eat."

"There is wisdom in your words," said Jan. "Let us search for food and a boat."

CHAPTER XIX

THE RIVER OF MONSTERS

AT FIRST THEY were undecided whether to go up the river to the west, or down the river to the east. Behind them to the north was the Temple of Set, with its cluster of buildings and its background of pyramid-shaped mausoleums. The main temple housed the High Priest, his black-robed assistants and attendants, and his black-armored warriors.

In a group of smaller buildings lived the tradesmen, artisans, and laborers, comprising a small village with its market place. And in a tiny cluster of hovels near the Temple of Sebek were the despised handlers of the dead—the embalmers, who spent their lives segregated from other men. They had no intercourse with others except to receive the bodies intended for the burial grounds of Set, and to return the embalmed mummies to the temple attendants, who placed them in the caskets.

The nobles of Set lived in baronial castles scattered about the country north of the temple, where peasants toiled in fields and tended flocks. Koh had explained these things to Jan, so both knew that it would be extremely dangerous for them to venture north, away from the river.

Across the river to the south was the magnificent City of Satmu, capital of the empire. It was in the center of an island about five miles by ten, rimmed by marshes and a circle of rolling, partly wooded areas. Four immense arch bridges connected the island with the mainland to the north, south, east and west, each bridge guarded by a small fortress. The city itself was circular, and about three miles in diameter. From where they stood on the river bank the two fugitives could see its north wall, and beyond that its gayly colored roof tops, its towers, domes and minarets.

Standing in the center of the city, and dominating the scene with its great size and magnificence was the Imperial Palace, its central dome of polished gold reflecting the rays of the afternoon sun with dazzling brilliance.

SINCE THE north bridge lay only a mile to the east of them, Koh and Jan decided to go toward the west. They had not gone far when the jungle-trained Jan suddenly caught his companion by the arm and cautioned silence. Koh could hear or see nothing at first, but presently he heard the rustle of small animals through the undergrowth and the patter of their little feet. Jan had not heard them much sooner than his friend, but his delicately attuned nostrils had caught their scent long before the sound was audible.

Motioning to Koh to remain where he was, Jan swiftly and noiselessly swung himself up into the tangle of branches and lianas above. In less than a minute he was directly above a herd of small, spotted animals, none of them much bigger than a full=grown fox, and bearing a singular resemblance to the horses which he had seen on some of the plantations that fringed his jungle. Their scent, too, was singularly like that of horses. He remembered having seen a picture of one of these creatures in Ramona's book of extinct animals. It was called an eohippus, and she had told him it was the earliest known ancestor of the horse.

Jan knew at a glance that the little beasts were not so dangerous as carnivorous beasts their size might have been, but still they might attack in mass if he should drop among them. Peccaries had done that several times, wounding him severely with their sharp teeth and hoofs and forcing him to take refuge in the trees, despite the fact that he was armed. And now he had no weapons whatever. But they must have meat.

Singling out his intended victim, Jan suddenly launched himself through the air with a throaty roar like that of an attacking puma, a sound which usually paralyzes the prey for an instant. As he alighted beside the little beast, Jan clutched it around the neck, while the rest of the herd, squealing with fright, splashed up the bank and plunged into the undergrowth.

With a deft twist, Jan broke the neck of the prize. Then he swung it over his shoulder and walked back to where Koh waited for him.

"Here's our meat," he said, and proudly displayed his kill.

"But we have no knife to cut it with, and no fire," objected Koh.

"What of that?" asked Jan. "We have our teeth and hands. The meat is fresh and good. Cooking would only spoil it."

He tore off a foreleg and handed it, still dripping with warm blood, to his companion. Then he tore off another, and peeling back the hide as an ape peels a banana, began devouring the tender flesh with gusto. Koh, the delicately nurtured prince of an ancient civilization, held the gory portion handed him as if it had been a burning brand, and watched Jan with wonder and a tinge of horror.

"By the long red feathers of Kan!" he exclaimed. "I have heard that the hairy ones, the man-apes who live in the caves so devour their meat, but never have I seen nor heard of a man eating it thus."

"And never," said Jan, "have I tasted such sweet and delicious meat. Try it."

"I'll starve first," said Koh, and flung his portion to the ground.

JAN MADE no reply, but continued eating, squatting on his haunches and gazing out over the river toward the distant golden dome where he hoped to find and rescue Chicma. Presently a small sailing vessel hove into view. It had a single, lateen sail of golden yellow hue, in the center of which was painted a coat of arms. There were three men in the boat, and a pile of recently slain water birds.

"The emperor's fowlers," whispered Koh. "That is one of the boats that supplies the imperial table with the birds that inhabit the marshes."

"How do they kill them?" asked Jan, seeing no weapons in evidence.

"With throwing sticks," replied Koh. "See, each man has a small pile of curved sticks beside him. I have heard that the emperor himself sometimes hunts thus, for the sport of the thing."

As Koh watched Jan, eating with apparent relish, his hunger increased. Finally it overcame his scruples, and he picked up the leg which he had cast away so disdainfully. Following Jan's example, he first peeled back a portion of the skin. Then he shut his eyes, and tearing off a bite, quickly chewed and swallowed it. Much to his surprise, he really liked it.

By this time Jan had devoured most of the meat on his portion, and was gnawing the gristly parts of the joints, which he swallowed with relish. Then he cracked the bones between his strong teeth and ate the marrow for desert. These things he had learned to do by watching the carnivores of the jungle, and having once tried them, had found them to his liking.

Having satisfied his hunger, Jan went down to the river to wash his face and hands, and to drink. Then he returned, and with that feeling of contentment which follows a satisfying and tasty meal, lay down to doze in the speckled shade and to wait for Koh to finish. For the first time since his capture by the black-robes, life was once more worth living.

Koh was not long about finishing his meal. When he had washed and drunk at the river, Jan sprang to his feet and slung the remains of his kill over his shoulder. They started off along the river bank to the west.

The sloping, jungle-draped shore gradually gave way to a steeper and more rocky formation, where the vegetation, except for a narrow fringe of willows and oleanders at the water's edge, was quite sparse. Soon they were picking their way among fallen boulders and rock fragments at the base of a steep bluff.

Suddenly Jan, who was in the lead, stopped and sniffed the air apprehensively. Koh came to a halt behind him, peering around his shoulder in an attempt to learn the cause for his uneasiness.

But the cause announced itself with unexpected and terrifying suddenness. For, with a terrific roar that rolled across the river valley, a great shaggy creature crept from a cave mouth about ten feet above Jan's head, and with its claws aspread and white teeth gleaming, tensed to launch its mighty bulk through the air straight for the startled youths.

CHAPTER XX

MAN-HUNT

THE MORNING AFTER his arrival at the hacienda, Dr. Bracken was astir bright and early. After drinking a cup of coffee and declining all items of breakfast which the obsequious butler suggested, he lighted a black stogie and strolled outdoors. The sun was rising with a blaze of glory, swiftly dissipating the mists that hung over the river, and promising an exceptionally warm day.

As the doctor made his way toward the huts where his Indians were quartered, he caught sight of a familiar figure standing on the dock and gazing out over the river—Captain Santos. He immediately turned his steps in that direction.

Santos looked around as a board creaked beneath the doctor's tread.

"Ah, good morning, captain!" greeted the doctor. "Up early, I see."

"*Sí.* Eet was no use to stay in bed. I could not sleep wan weenk all night. I 'ave fall een love to beat hal'. I can't sleep, I can't eat, for theenk about that keed."

"The best thing you can do," said the doctor, "is to snap out of it *muy pronto,* and work with me. Now—how many of our Indians can we trust with this work, provided they are well paid?"

Santos grinned. "We can trust any of them—eef well paid."

"Then here's the plan: We have thirty Indians, all told. I gather that this wild boy is somewhere in the jungles to the

121

south of here. I think I know where to find him and how to capture him. After he is caught, I must have a place to keep him until I am ready to bring him here.

"So we'll split into three searching parties. We'll allot ten men to Trevor, and let him go to the north, where he'll be quite sure not to find Jan. You will take ten men and head east, while I go south with the other ten. Instead of Continuing east, however, you will circle southward until you strike my trail. I'll wait for you at my first camp. Then I'll show you where I want you to build my little prison. We'll make a secret base camp on the spot, and we'll take Jan there:

"Your plans, *señor*, are good for your own ends. What about mine?"

"I was coming to that. Once we get Jan we'll see that a message from him reaches the girl, asking her to meet him at a certain place. She'll go. Well have two Indians there to persuade her to go the rest of the way to our camp. If something goes wrong with our plans we'll kill the Indians for attempted abduction. Their comrades will not know they have been paid to do this work, and dead men tell no tales.

"*Señor,*" said Santos, admiringly, "you 'ave wan damn' good head. What you say, I do."

"Good. Get your three parties organized, and I'll go and fix things with Trevor."

DR. BRACKEN found the Trevors breakfasting with the don and doña. He outlined his plan to them, and all were in hearty accord with it. Don Fernando offered to take ten of his own men and search' the country to the west, across the river, though Jan had never been known to hunt in that part of the jungle and that was agreed upon.

By ten o'clock the four bands were ready to march. Farewells were being said. The two, women were saying good-bye to their husbands, while the doctor and Ramona stood a little way off.

Suddenly, to Dr. Bracken's surprise, she turned to him and said in a low voice:

"I'll tell you something, doctor, if you will promise not to tell anyone."

"Eh? Of course I'll promise, *señorita.*"

She came closer. "It's about Jan. I believe I can tell you where to find him. You see, my father and mother don't know that he came to see me many times after he saved me from the puma. But I do so want you to find him and bring him back!"

"I'll find him, never fear," replied the doctor, "even if I have to devote my whole life to it. What was it you were going to say?"

"He told me," said Ramona, "that he lived in a tree-hut, four days' journey to the south. It is beside a deep pool that is beneath a waterfall. Your chimpanzee is there, also. That is all I know, but it may help."

"It will help a lot," the doctor assured her, "and I am deeply grateful to you for confiding in me. You may rest assured that your confidence has not been misplaced. And now the others are ready, so I will say good-bye."

The doctor smiled grimly to himself as he led his band of Indians away. This was going to be easier than he had anticipated. In one of his packs was a case of hypodermic needle cartridges, such as he had used for capturing wild animals in Africa. After finding Jan's tree, all he would need to do would be to camp near it, out of sight, and wait for the young man to appear. A "hypo" bullet in the arm or leg would put him to sleep for several hours. When he awakened he would be in the doctor's power.

As for abducting Ramona, Dr. Bracken had no intention of carrying out this part of the bargain with his confederates. He could easily dispose of Santos in the jungle, and return to the hacienda with the report that the captain had been killed by a native's blow-gun dart.

The doctor was in an excellent humor when, about an hour before sunset, he bade his Indians halt and make camp. He had finished his evening meal and lighted a stogie when Santos and his Indians marched into camp.

The two bands camped together that night, and together went forward on the following day, and for two days thereafter. Then, as night was drawing near, Dr. Bracken heard the roar of a waterfall. Bidding the Indians stop where they were and make camp, he took Santos forward with him. Before he left, he loaded his rifle with a hypo cartridge and ordered the captain to do the same.

THEY LOCATED the waterfall about a half mile away. Looking upward, the doctor, with a grin of triumph, saw Jan's tree house.

"Wait here and keep out of sight," ordered the doctor, "while I go forward to investigate. If the man or the ape shows up, shoot for an arm or leg."

He handed the captain several extra hypo cartridges and walked over beneath Jan's tree. Beneath it he found many nut-shells, the dried remains of orange, pineapple and banana skins, and a number of gnawed bones. The appearance of these remains convinced him that neither Jan nor the ape had been in the tree for several months.

He accordingly laid his rifle on the grass, and climbed the tree. Perspiring in every pore and breathing heavily, he presently reached the lowest limb and drew himself up on it.

A single glance into the interior of the hut convinced him that it had not been used for some time. With great curiosity, he examined Jan's collection of native weapons, ornaments, clothing and hides. Careful woodsman that he was, he looked also for evidence that would convince him beyond any doubt that this was Jan's hut. With the aid of his flash light he found it, clinging to the bark of the tree trunk—chimpanzee hair, auburn hair, and the hair rubbed from the jaguar skin garments with which Borno had clothed both of them.

He was about to leave when he noticed something else—a piece of notebook paper projecting from beneath a badly cured jaguar skin. Quickly lifting the pelt, he saw many more pieces of paper and a stubby, much-chewed pencil. The papers were covered with pencil drawings, crude but showing marks of talent, and with much childish printing, all in capital letters. In it he found many names and descriptions of animals, both prehistoric and existing, evidently copied from natural histories. He also found the sentence written over and over: "Jan likes Ramona."

Pocketing one of the papers and replacing the skin over the others, the doctor, quite satisfied with his discoveries, climbed down the tree once more. Picking up his rifle, he walked over to where Santos awaited him.

"I've found his lair," he said. "Some day, if he is alive, he is sure to return to it. We'll build a blind, here at the edge of the jungle, and post a good marksman in it night and day, with a rifle and plenty of hypo cartridges. While we're waiting for the lad to return we can be building our cell and our permanent camp."

"You are sure this ees the right place?"

"Positive. Look here." The doctor extracted the folded note paper from his pocket and handed it to Santos.

"So! What ees this? A beeg bone-backed lizard weeth teeth on his back and horns on his tail. 'Stegosaurus,' eet say onderneath."

"A prehistoric reptile," said the doctor. "Jan must have copied it from one of Ramona's books."

"*Mil demonios!* You theenk he steal her book? Eet say here, too, 'Jan likes Ramona.' *Carramba!* I geeve him a real bullet if I catch him fool around her!"

"If you give him anything but a hypo bullet before I'm through with him, it will be just too bad for you," warned the doctor, snatching the paper from his hand. "When I have finished with him you can chop him in little pieces, for all I care, but not before. *Sabe?*"

"*Sí, señor,* I onderstand. But after that he better look out, I tal' you."

Darkness came on with the suddenness common to the

tropics just as they got to camp, so nothing more could be done
that day.

EARLY THE next morning the doctor left minute instructions
with Santos for the construction of the jail cell and permanent
camp, and took two Indians with him to build the blind near
the tree-hut.

Having finished the blind; the doctor left the two Indians
on guard there, promising to send two more that night to relieve
them. Each was armed with a rifle containing a hypo cartridge,
and ordered to shoot only for the arm or leg.

A week later the permanent camp was completed. There was
a cabin for the doctor and Santos, in one end of which a small
room was partitioned off by means of stout wooden bars. This,
the doctor called his *carcel*, or jail, and it was here that he intended to imprison Jan until he should be ready to take part in
the terrible climax to his revenge which he head planned and
toward which end his life, since the birth of the boy, had been
devoted with a fervor worthy of a better cause.

There was also a bunk house and cook shack for the Indians.

But while all this was taking place, Santos was doing a certain
amount of planning in the furtherance of his own ends. It was
not necessary, he thought, to capture Jan in order to entice
Ramona away from the hacienda. This could easily be done by
sending her a short note imitating Jan's writing.

Without broaching his plan to the doctor, whom he knew
would frown on it because it might interfere with his own
scheme, Santos took two of his Indians into his confidence,
offering each an immense sum of money for his part in the
crime. Soon it would be necessary to send some one back to
the hacienda for supplies, and when this time came he meant
to detail his two accomplices for the work.

CHAPTER XXI

FORBIDDEN GROUND

AT THE THUNDEROUS roar of the beast just above their heads, about to spring, Jan and Koh both leaped forward as if propelled by a powerful springboard, and ran as fast as they could. There was the thud of an immense body on the spot they had just vacated, followed by the gallop of huge pads and the rattle of long claws on the stones.

They had not gone far when Jan knew, by the increasing proximity of the sounds from behind, that the great beast was rapidly gaining on them. He threw a quick glance over his shoulder, and recognized it instantly from a picture he had seen in Ramona's book—a giant cave bear.

Knowing that further flight was useless, and that unarmed as he was he would be quickly pulled down and devoured, he decided to stake everything on the chance that he might be able to outwit this terrible enemy. Suddenly halting in his tracks, he turned and faced his pursuer.

The bear instantly came to a sliding halt, alert for a trap or ambush. When it appeared to have satisfied itself that no hunters lurked nearby, and that it was confronted only by a single unarmed man—for Koh had continued his running, not knowing that Jan had stopped—it reared up on its hind legs, head and shoulders taller than a tall man, and advanced, roaring thunderously.

Jan raised the carcass of the little eohippus over his head, then hurled it straight at the oncoming beast. It just grazed one furry ear and alighted some ten feet behind the bear. But in the instant of its passing the monster had got a whiff of its favorite food, the elusive but toothsome little dawn horse.

Suddenly dropping to all fours, the bear turned arid started toward the carcass. Jan took advantage of this by adding to the distance between himself and the monster. The beast heard him and swung about again, undecided whether to take the game already killed or pursue that which was still alive.

But the bear was not the only carnivore in the vicinity that had scented freshly killed eohippus. A slinking, dog-like beast came trotting down the trail, sniffing hungrily, and keeping a wary eye on the bear. The latter did not hear it until it loosened a small stone. Then it swung about with a snail.

The presence of the new brute, which Jan recognized as a hyaenodon, decided the issue. With a fierce roar of rage, the bear sprang for the intruder just as it was about to seize the prize. The hyaenodon leaped back out of reach of the great, flailing claws, and squatted on its haunches. It could not hope to get a full meal now, but it would wait with doglike patience until the bear had finished, hoping that the lordly beast might leave a few edible scraps.

Jan did not wait to see more, but hurried on after his companion. He found Koh coming toward him a few hundred feet down the trail.

"I missed you," said the prince, "and so came back, fearing the bear had caught you."

"There is still danger," said Jan. "I gave it the eohippus, but that will only be a mouthful for such a big brute. Come on."

THEY SET off at a stiff trot, which either of the youths was capable of keeping up for hours. Presently Koh stopped and caught his companion's arm.

"Look!" he cried, excitedly. "A boat!"

The sun was dropping behind the tree-clothed river bluffs as they hurried down the bank to examine their prize: It was only a crude dugout canoe with one paddle and a barbed, three-pronged fishing spear lying in the bottom. But to these two it was as welcome as the most luxurious and palatial yacht.

"Get in the other end," said Koh. "I'll push off."

Jan did as he was bidden. He had had no experience with canoes except as a passenger, and bowed to his friend's superior knowledge and skill.

Koh lifted the anchor, a stone with a rope around it, into the boat. Then he pushed off, scrambled aboard, and seized the paddle.

He had not taken two strokes when there came an angry shout from the river bank. A bearded, sun-bronzed white man, naked save for breech-clout and sandals, ran down to the water's edge and launched a long spear at them. It flew high, but Jan stood up and caught it.

"Come back, thieves!" shouted the man on the bank. "Come back, cowards, and I will kill you with my bare hands!"

Koh was using the paddle with considerable dexterity.

"Too bad to take his boat," he said. "Evidently he is a fisherman, and this is his means of livelihood." He shouted over his shoulder to the raging man on the bank. "We'll leave your boat on the island for you—straight across. Come over the bridge and get it."

In reply, the man hurled after them a choice collection of Satmuan curses. Then the darkness descended suddenly, and he faded from view.

Koh was an expert with the paddle, and it did not take him long to reach the opposite shore. The prow grounded among some rushes, and Jan, leaping out, dragged it up until more than half of the boat was out of the water. He retained the spear which the bearded man had cast at him, and Koh followed with the fishing spear.

For some time they splashed through a grassy marsh. Presently they struck higher ground, and entered a thick, dark wood. Here were many strange smells and sounds. Great beasts crashed through, the scents of which were totally unfamiliar to

Jan. Weird cries, shrieks, bellows and roars resounded in the darkness, unlike anything he had ever heard in his own jungle. These made him cautious, so he progressed but slowly.

Koh had never been in the jungle at night before, and though he was a brave youth his nerves were constantly on edge at each new noise. He was following Jan, holding onto the butt of his spear, so they would not become separated in the inky darkness.

There were mighty, flesh-eating killers abroad in the jungle. No mistake about that. From time, to time they heard the plaintive death cries of helpless creatures dragged down by carnivores, and the struggles' of others.

WITH IMMENSE relief they emerged from the jungle about midnight. The moon had risen, and they saw through a ten-foot barricade of heavy posts, set about four inches apart, a rolling plain covered with short grass. Busily cropping this grass with their parrot-like beaks, singly and in scattered groups, were several hundred of the terrible, three-horned mounts of the Satmuans.

One triceratops grazing near them evidently heard them or caught their scent, for it lowered its immense head and charged belligerently, clear up to the paling. There it stopped, snorting and pawing the earth.

"It looks as if we will have to go around this pasture," said Koh. "I'd rather go back into that dark jungle than climb in there with those brutes."

"If they are so fierce, how is it that the soldiers and hunters can ride them?" asked Jan.

"They learn to know their masters and their masters' people," replied Koh. "They are fighting beasts, you know, ridden by fighting men, and to them all strangers are enemies. Unless restrained by their riders, they will attack any strangers they meet. These beasts are quite docile among Satmuans, but they attack strangers, and will even attack other beasts of their own kind belonging to strangers."

As they circled the pasture near the paling, the immense

brute inside kept pace with their progress. But presently tiring of this, or perhaps convinced that they were not going to enter, it left them with a contemptuous snort, to return to its feeding.

At last Jan and Koh drew near to a long row of low sheds, near which were a number of small, round buildings with lights shining from their windows.

"The stables," said Koh, "and the houses of the keepers."

They circled once more, this time through a grove of orange trees planted in straight rows. This brought them up against the northwest wall of the city—a wall fifty feet high, smooth and unscalable. At intervals of five hundred feet along this wall were guard towers, in each of which was a sentinel.

"Well, here we are," whispered Koh, "This is as far as I can guide you. I don't know of any way we can get into the city except as prisoners."

"There must be some way," said Jan. "Let us look."

They circled to the left, keeping to the shadow of the wall so they would not be seen from above, until they were scarcely a quarter of a mile from the great, arched north gate. This Koh assured Jan, had been closed for the night, and would be guarded by not less than fifty men.

CHAPTER XXII

A PERILOUS VISIT

AS THEY STOOD there talking, Jan took hold of a thick creeper which bad grown up the side of the wall, and pulled it to throw it out of his way. To his surprise, it clung to the wall. He pulled harder, but it would not budge. Then he stepped away from the wall and looked upward. Half a dozen creepers like this one had climbed side by side, almost to the summit.

"Come!" he whispered to Koh. "Here is a way into the city."

Tearing off a branch of the vine, he made both ends fast to the hunting spear and slung it over his back that he might have the use of both hands. Koh did likewise with the fishing spear. Then Jan sprang up the vine with ape-like agility, and the prince, after waiting until they were about twenty feet apart in order that their combined, weight would not be on the same tendrils at the same time, followed.

When he reached the top of the wall, Jan moved with extreme caution. His position was about halfway between two sentry towers. The sentry on his left was standing in front of the tower, leaning on his longbow and looking out toward the bridge. At first he could not see the one on his right, but he presently made out his huddled form leaning against the tower, asleep.

Very carefully, Jan drew himself up, and flattening, wormed across the edge of the wall. It was about three feet thick at the upper edge. Just behind it was a row of terraces, each three feet wide, and with a drop of the same distance to the next, reaching clear to the ground. He crawled down onto the first terrace and unslinging his spear, waited. In a moment he was joined by Koh, and the two noiselessly descended the terraces until they reached the ground.

The part of the city in which they found themselves was a residence section of flat-roofed buildings set closely together, their fronts level with the paved street. Lights showed in a few of the houses, but most of them were dark, showing that their occupants had retired.

After following the wall for some distance, they came to a narrow street, lighted only by the rays of the moon, and now nearly deserted.

"This street must lead to the palace," said Koh, "for I have heard that the city is laid out like the web of a spider, with streets branching out in all directions, but all centered at the Imperial Palace. The palace, with its gold dome, represents the sun, and the streets branching out from it, the rays. There are concentric circles of narrower streets connecting the ray streets."

"Then let us follow this street," said Jan.

"Dressed as we are," replied Koh, "that would be an impossibility. The streets are constantly patrolled and we would be seen and captured."

"And where would we be taken?"

"Probably to the palace for judgment. Ordinary prisoners would be taken before a magistrate, but because I am of royal blood and you are a stranger in the valley we would probably be taken before the emperor, himself."

"After all," mused Jan, "it would be the easiest way to get there."

"What do you mean?"

"Leave your spear here and follow me."

JAN DISCARDED his hunting spear and started down the street. Koh dropped the fishing spear and followed. The first person they passed wore the garb of a merchant. He stared at them as if he could not believe his eyes, but they walked on, ignoring him.

They saw two more men approaching. Moonlight glinted from their polished armor and the tips of their spears.

"The patrol!" whispered Koh.

"Good!" replied Jan.

He swaggered straight toward the oncoming figures. Koh followed his example. Soon the clank of armor and weapons was audible. It grew louder. Jan thought the two would pass them by, unnoticed, but suddenly as they were abreast, one turned.

"Halt!" he commanded.

Jan and Koh stopped in their tracks. The two in armor sauntered over, peering at them.

"A strange pair," said the first, staring beneath his raised visor.

"By the long slim beak of Tehuti!" exclaimed the other. "A savage dressed in the skin of an animal!"

"And this other!" said the first. "Pierce me through, if he wears not the scarlet of the royal house of Kan! Who are you two?" he demanded:

"I am Koh of Temukan," said the prince.

"And I am Jan."

"Jan of where? Of what?"

The youth hesitated for a moment.

"Jan of the jungle," he replied.

"Of the jungle? You look the part. Where are you going?"

"We were on our way to the palace."

"To the palace! You hear him, Batau? They were going to the palace—a jungle savage and a yellow prince! No doubt they intended calling on his imperial majesty, the emperor."

"No doubt, Pebek. They are visiting royalty—a prince of Temukan and a prince of the jungle. It would be discourteous to let them go unattended."

"They should have a guard of honor. We will go with them to the palace." Pebek bowed ironically to the two youths. "You will permit us to escort you. Proceed."

The two youths moved forward, each with a spear point at his back.

On their way to the palace they met a few straggling towns-men. These stared, but made no comment. Soon they stood before the great arched gate of the palace grounds. Here were fully fifty golden-armored warriors on guard. Jan began to realize the magnitude of the task he had undertaken.

At a word from their captors the gates swung open, and they were allowed to pass.

"This place is easier gotten into than out of," muttered Koh.

"So it seems," replied Jan, "but we are not ready to leave, yet."

"Silence you two," growled Batau, and prodded Jan with his spear point.

WITH THE pain of that wound, Jan's carefully thought out plan was forgotten. It transformed him, in an instant, to a raging jungle creature.

He whirled with a snarl of rage and, seizing the shaft of the spear, snapped it off. Balancing it for a moment, he hurled the resulting three-foot javelin with all his might. It struck Batau in the left eye and entered his brain, killing him instantly.

Pebek had attempted to come to the rescue of his comrade, but he had immediately been set upon by Koh. His movements impeded by the weight of his armor, the warrior was far too slow for his agile adversary. He had dropped his long spear, useless at such close quarters, and was drawing his sword, when Koh snatched his dagger from his belt and struck for his neck, just above the rim of his breast plate. The slim blade went home to the jugular, and Pebek, after staggering blindly for a moment, slumped to the ground, blood oozing from between the joints of his armor.

"Quick!" pasted Koh. "Let us get them out of sight. If they are discovered the whole palace guard will be after us."

They swiftly dragged the two fallen warriors into the shrub-bery that bordered the path. Then they returned and picked up

the weapons that had been dropped, returning into the shrubbery with these.

Scarcely had they reached their place of concealment when
they heard the march of approaching warriors.

"They heard, and are after us," said Jan.

"I think not," replied Koh. "It is probably a squad from the
palace to relieve the watch at the gate. They keep step, and are
not hurrying. But when they reach the gate, look out."

Koh's surmise was proved correct, when a few moments later
fifty spear-men filed past, looking neither to the right nor left.
As soon as they had passed, each youth armed himself with the
sword and dagger of his fallen foe-man. Then they hurried away
toward the palace.

"How do you expect to find Chicma in that great building?"
asked Koh, as they stood in a little clump of tall trees, looking
up at the massive structure with its towers, turrets and balconies.

"By her scent, if she is there," replied Jan. He was looking up
at the tall tree beneath which they were standing. Its branches
brushed the railing of an upper balcony.

AT THIS moment there came a shout from the gate—the
sound of armed men running through the shrubbery.

"Follow me," said Jan. "I see a way into the palace, where
they will least expect to find us."

He sprang up into the tree, and climbed rapidly. The prince
followed more slowly, unable to compete with the ape-like
agility of his companion. When he reached the limb that
brushed the balcony, Jan swung out on it, caught the railing,
and drew himself up. At the rear of the balcony a hinged
window stood open. The room behind it was in darkness.

Creeping over to the opening, Jan investigated the room with
twitching, sensitive nostrils. His nose told him that people had
been there recently, but that it was unoccupied now. Koh came
silently over the railing.

Excited shouts came up to them from the ground, cries of
rage. The two bodies had been discovered.

Jan led the way into the darkened room. At the far end, he saw a faint blur of light, and went directly toward this. It came from behind a heavy curtain which draped a doorway. Cautiously he moved the curtain a little way. Outside was a narrow hall, lighted at intervals by lamps hung on wall brackets. The oil burning in them gave off a mild, sweet aroma that reminded Jan of flowers.

A quick survey showed him that there was no one in the hall. He stepped out, followed by Koh, his nostrils wide as he endeavored to catch Chicma's scent. The perfume from the lamps confused him.

Presently he turned to the left and like a hound on a trail, went straight to a door about fifty feet away. Here he halted, sniffing for a moment, then lifted the curtain and peered in.

He saw Chicma, but she was not in a cage, and she was not alone. She was lolling on a cushioned divan, daintily nibbling on a sweetmeat from a dish piled high on a taboret beside her. Her ragged jaguar-skin garment was gone. In its place was a gaudily colored jacket of the softest silk. There was a jewel-studded gold collar around her neck, and jewels blazed from golden settings on her finger and toe rings. Beside her stood a slender yellow slave girl, who was brushing her fur.

Jan turned to Koh.

"Seize the slave," he whispered. "We'll bind and gag her. Then Chicma can come away with us."

Together they rushed in. Koh clapped his hand over the girl's mouth before she could cry out. Startled by their abrupt entrance, Chicma leaped down from the divan and started to run. Then she recognized Jan, and stopped.

"What do you want?" she clucked, in her guttural chimpanzee tongue.

"I've come to take you away," he said.

"I like it here," she replied. "I won't go away. You do not need me. You are grown, and can care for yourself. Go away and don't bother me."

JAN WAS dumfounded. To think that he had risked his life needlessly, passed through countless perils to save Chicma from her captors, only to find that she actually liked her captivity! All this he could not tell to Chicma. There was no chimpanzee way of expressing it.

"I will go," he clucked to her. To Koh: "She won't go. We must go without her. First I'll help you bind the girl."

He tore a strip of cloth from the curtain. But before he could use it, the girl suddenly wrenched her mouth free from Koh's hand, and shrieked loudly.

There was an answering shout from the hallway, the clank of armored men running.

"No use to bind her now," said Jan. "Come."

He dashed out the window, onto the balcony. Koh flung the girl from him and followed, just as a host of warriors rushed into the room. One of the guards, searching the shrubbery beneath, spied the two figures on the balcony and shouting to his fellows, pointed upward.

The nearest tree stood about twenty feet from the balcony. Jan stepped up on the rail, and shouting, "Follow me!" plunged across the dizzy height. For him it was not much of a jump. Many times he had leaped this far, from tree to tree, in the jungle. His sure hands gripped the lowest branch, clung there. But the branch cracked, sagged, then tore loose from the trunk. Jan's body swung out to the horizontal and dropped. He struck on his back with terrific force. Then came oblivion.

CHAPTER XXIII

THE LOTUS MARK

IN HER BOUDOIR on the second floor of the Suarez hacienda, Doña Isabella was talking with Georgia Trevor. The hour of the siesta was past and a servant had just brought tea.

Ramona, accompanied by her duenna, bad gone quietly to the patio to read a book.

Jan had not been found. After two months in the jungle Dr. Bracken had sent word that he had set up a base camp far to the south, and that he had sent a messenger to Captain Santos, instructing him to build a similar camp to the east. He bad suggested that the same thing be done to the north and west thus keeping a large area of the jungle under constant watch. Harry Trevor, trusting him implicitly, had immediately accepted the plan. Both he and Don Fernando were absent, establishing the new base camps, but were expected to return that day, as Ramona was to leave for school early the following morning.

Georgia Trevor stirred her tea thoughtfully. "Ramona seems quite sad today," she said. "I wonder what can be wrong with her? Do you think it is because her vacation has ended and she must leave for the States tomorrow?"

The doña put down her cup. "That may have something to do with it," she answered. "But she has assured me many times that she likes school. There is something wrong with Ramona, some undercurrent I can't fathom. At the beginning of her

*He thrust the rude spear straight
at the thunder bird's beak.*

vacation she was bright and cheerful, but as the days passed she seemed to grow more and more worried about something."

"She's still quite young to be away from home for ten months at a time," suggested Georgia Trevor. "No doubt she gets homesick. Only seventeen, isn't she?"

"Yes—er—we think she is. I may as well tell you all about it," said the doña. "Ramona is not our daughter, though we love and cherish her as our very own."

"I've noticed that except for her dark eyes and hair she doesn't resemble either you or Don Fernando. There seems to be something Oriental about her type of beauty, suggesting a princess of ancient Babylon or a vestal virgin from some temple of Isis."

"It may be," said the doña, "that your intuition is nearer the troth than you realize. I'll show you something."

SHE OPENED a tiny wall safe and from one of its trays removed a large brass key. With this she unlocked the lid of a massive brass-bound chest. In the bottom of the chest was a black lacquered basket, its lid inscribed in white, red and yellow, with characters greatly resembling Egyptian hieroglyphics. As if it were a fragile sacred relic, the doña lifted it reverently and placed it on a table.

"This," said the doña, "is the basket in which we found Ramona a tiny baby not more than six months old. My husband had gone out on the river with an Indian servant, for some early morning fishing. He noticed the basket floating nearby, and was attracted by the strange characters with which it was covered.

"He lifted the basket into the boat, and was astounded when he heard strange little mewling sounds coming from it. He tore off the lid. Lying in the bottom of the basket on a bed of soft wool, wrapped in a shawl of golden-yellow silk, was a tiny baby girl.

"He rushed home to me at once, and when I saw the child, I immediately fell in love with her. She was half starved, showing that she had been floating in the basket for many hours. She may have traveled that way for a great many miles, as the current is very swift. We tried to learn who her parents were, and when we were not able to find out anything about them, we adopted her.

"The inscriptions on the basket could not be read by any of the Indians we asked, although for some reason the Indians always seemed to regard them with superstitious awe.

"About a year later Sir Henry Westgate, the English archaeologist and explorer, stopped here on his way into the jungle. He told us he sought traces of colonists from an ancient civilization that had once existed on a vast continent in the Pacific.

"My husband showed him this basket, told him where and how he had found it, and asked if he could decipher the writing on it. Sir Henry's expression when he saw that basket reminded me of Galahad, finding the Holy Grail. He said that it was a historical discovery of vast importance, and that if the people who had set it adrift could be located, the riddle of the lost continents of Mu, Atlantis and Lemuria and the origins of all ancient civilizations and cultures could be solved. Here is his translation."

FROM THE bottom of the basket she took a sheet of paper, and read aloud:

"'To thee, mighty Hepr, Great God of the Waters, enthroned in eternal power and glory upon the coils of the great serpent, between thy sentinels the twin mountains Qer-Hapi and Mu-Hapi, Samsu, humble slave of thy beloved son, Set, consigneth this daughter of Re, that thou mayest deal with her in thy great wisdom according to thy omnipotent will so powerful that went thou to relax it for but an instant, the gods would fall down headlong and all men would perish.'"

"What can it mean?" asked Georgia Trevor, tensely.

"According to Sir Henry," replied the doña, "it means that a certain Samsu, High Priest of Set, or Saturn, for some reason set the child adrift upon the water, hoping that she would meet her death. She may have been his own child, or she may have been the daughter of some other powerful man. The statement that she is a daughter of Re shows that she is a royal princess, or daughter of the sun. For the safety of his soul even though he desired her death, the High Priest dared not slay a royal personage himself. So I suppose he managed to put the blame on Hepr, God of Waters, by consigning her to the river in a basket that would float.

"In the palm of the baby's right hand was tattooed an open lotus, the sacred flower of Mu. This proved beyond all doubt that Ramona was a princess of the blood imperial, Sir Henry said. If he is correct, Ramona's ancestors were ruling a mighty civilization while our Cro-Magnon forbears in Europe were living in caves and wearing animal skins.

"The remains of every civilization of the past, Sir Henry told us, show the cultural influence of Mu, the mother continent. Her ships carried adventurers to all parts of the earth, where they established colonies ruled by the viceroys of the motherland. But Mu, along with Lemuria was broken up by a great earthquake, and sank into the ocean.

"An expedition had set out from the motherland on a good-will tour of Mu's colonies, led by the Crown Prince, with a retinue of ten thousand men and women from all walks of life.

"While he was in Egypt the prince received word of the destruction of the motherland. He set sail for Atlantis, but in a terrific storm many of his ships were lost. Of his own flagship nothing was ever heard.

"Sir Henry was convinced that the prince and a band of his followers had landed somewhere on the coast of South America. The sight of Ramona's basket convinced him that he was on the right trail, and that if he would follow this river and all of its branches to their sources, he would be sure to find the descendants of the people of Mu. With this intention he led an expedition into the jungle some sixteen years ago. Since then no word has come from him. Probably he and his men were killed by savages."

STANDING IN the patio beneath the tiny balcony that jutted out from the doña's boudoir, Ramona waited for Jan. She had waited there every day of her vacation, but now, the last day, hope had fled.

A humming bird with iridescent plumage shot past Ramona's head as she sat beneath the trysting tree, and lighted on a bush, beneath the doña's window. She put down her book and followed it, to watch it at close range while it sipped the nectar from the flowers.

Above the pixie drone of the midget flyer's wings, she suddenly heard her supposed mother say: "Ramona is not our daughter." Shocked, she had remained to listen, and had heard the whole story.

Ramona turned away from the window with eyes brimming, stunned to, learn that she was not a Suarez and that the don and doña, whom she had loved as her father and mother, had merely taken her in, a foundling. Her real parents, it seemed, had not wanted her—had even desired her death. Otherwise they would not have set her adrift on the river where the chances were a hundred to one that she would perish.

As she walked down the path toward her tree, an Indian entered the patio. He glanced cautiously about as if fearful of being seen, then came toward her. Bowing low, he handed the girl a folded slip of paper.

"Jan send you this," he said softly, with a wary glance in the direction of the snoring duenna. "I wait for you outside gate."

With' trembling, eager fingers, Ramona unfolded the little missive, while the Indian slunk away. She instantly recognized the large, crudely made capital letters of Jan's writing.

> RAMONA:
> I AM BADLY HURT. WANT TO SEE YOU. THE IN-
> DIAN WILL SHOW THE WAY. WILL YOU COME?
> JAN.

Would she go? She had promised her father that she would never leave the patio, unguarded. No, not her father. Don Fernando had deceived her about that, as had the doña. Yet a promise was a promise, for all that, and she had never broken her word.

For a moment she stood there, a prey to conflicting emotions. But only for a moment. This was an emergency. Jan was wounded—perhaps dying. And he wanted to see her—needed her. That was enough. Promise or no promise, she must go.

As she passed the arbor, the corpulent Señora Soledade stirred uneasily, ceased her snoring for a moment, and seemed about to awaken. Ramona ran forward on tiptoes and quietly opened the gate. Stepping through she closed it soundlessly. Over among the young rubber trees the Indian stood with folded arms, waiting.

When he saw her coming, the savage started off toward the jungle. Once in its depths, he stopped until she came up.

"How far?" she asked.

"Only a little way," he answered. "I show you, quick."

At first he led her straight south, but presently he began turning toward the southeast. As they penetrated deeper and deeper into the jungle, Ramona began to grow apprehensive. She recalled that Jan had told her all Indians were his enemies. If this were the case, she wondered how it would be possible for him to employ an Indian as a messenger.

Then, to add to her fears, she began to hear sounds behind her, as if someone or something were dogging her footsteps. She ran up close to her guide—touched him on the shoulder.

"Something is following us," she said. "I heard it. It may be a puma or a jaguar. I'm afraid."

"I go look," said the savage, and walked back for a little way. Returning presently, he said: "Nothing follow. No be 'fraid."

He proceeded as before, but it was not long until the girl heard a twig snap behind her. She cast a quick glance over her shoulder, then screamed at the top of her voice as she saw a strange savage coming stealthily toward her, carrying a small coil of rope. Like a charging panther, the native sprang forward. She turned to run, but the Indian who had lured her into the jungle stopped her before she was fairly started. Then despite her cries and struggles, he held her while the other bound her hands and gagged her.

Then someone other than Jan had written the note! But who? And how could any one imitate his lettering so well?

SUDDENLY THEY came to a tiny clearing, walled in on all sides by tangled, matted vegetation. In the middle of the clearing was a small, newly built hut.

Standing in front of the hut, smoking a cigarette, was Captain Santos, a grin of triumph on his dark features. He dropped the butt, ground it beneath his heel, and slowly exhaled the blue-white smoke through his nostrils as the two Indians came up with their beautiful young captive.

"Unbind her," he commanded in Spanish.

While they loosed the bonds that held her wrists, the captain removed her gag.

"Now go! *Vamos!* Get the supplies from the hacienda and hurry back to camp. I'll see you there—later."

Ramona faced him bravely, trying to hide the horrible fear that clutched at her heart.

"What is the meaning of this, Captain Santos?" she demanded. "Where is Jan?"

"Jan," he replied, brutally seizing her wrists, "is dead. And since you ask, it means, my little one, that you are mine."

She tried to pull away, but the powerful fingers held her like steel bands. She kicked, bit and screamed, but Santos only laughed.

"Cry out all you like," he said. "It will amuse the monkeys and parrots." Then he dragged her into the dark interior of the hut.

CHAPTER XXIV

CAGED

WHEN JAN BECAME conscious after his fall from the tree, he was lying on a smooth stone floor. He sat up, and numerous twinges of pain shot through the muscles of his back.

Then he remembered his leap from the balcony of the Imperial Palace, the broken tree limb, and the crash that brought oblivion.

He got to his feet unsteadily and looked about. He was in a narrow cell, on all sides of which were stout iron bars. The air was heavy with the odors of sweating men and animals. In a cell on his right was a hairy man-monster like the ones that had attacked him when he first entered the valley. This husky creature was squatting in a corner, busily scratching himself. Jan could see other hairy monsters squatting in the cells beyond.

In the cell on Jan's left still another form paced back and forth. There were a few scattered patches of hair on his body, but the rest was quite naked and as white as Jan's own skin. His beard and the hair on his head were much longer than those of the hairy-bodied creatures at the right, both hanging below his waist, and were dark brown, streaked with gray. He stood more erect than these others, and was not nearly so heavy or muscular.

There were two doors to each cell. One led to a passageway in the rear, and the other to a circular arena of white sand about an eighth of a mile in diameter. Looking across this arena, and to the right and left, Jan could see hundreds of other cells. Those nearest him housed yellow men, white men, and hairy men. But in those farther away were caged many strange and terrible-looking creatures. Some, such as the saber-toothed tigers, cave bears and hyaenodons were familiar to him. But there were many others—giant beasts, birds, and reptiles—he had never seen or heard of before.

Presently a great commotion started among the men, beast-men, and beasts. Amid a deafening medley of roars, growls, shrieks, shouts and howls came a sound of clanging gates. Then Jan saw the reason. It was feeding time.

He could see the attendants coming along the passageway. One would move a lever, raising a gate a little way, while the other pushed food beneath it. Then the gate would clang back into place and the two would move on to the next cage while a third, following them, filled the water pans.

Like the beast-men on one side of him and the wild-looking white man on the other, Jan was fed raw meat. He was hungry, and seized it eagerly. It proved to be the flesh of some creature unfamiliar to him, but quite palatable and satisfying. After eating he drank, and lay down on his belly to ease his bruised and aching back. With his head cradled in his arms, he soon fell asleep.

SOME TIME later he awakened with a start. Something was prodding his shoulder. It was the end of a long pole thrust through the bars by a white man who wore a yellow tunic and sandals. He withdrew the pole as Jan scrambled to his feet and faced him.

"Do you speak the language of men, wild one?" he asked.

"When it pleases me," replied Jan defiantly.

The fellow grinned.

"It will do you no good to be surly with me," he said. "I am only here to help you. The games will start soon, and if you have the intelligence to listen and heed, so much the better for you."

"The games!" exclaimed Jan.

Then he remembered what Koh had said. If they were captured they would probably be sentenced to the games—to battle in the arena with men and monsters, usually against great odds. "Is Prince Koh here?" he asked.

"The prince is in the section with the other prisoners from Temukan," was the reply. "But heed me now, for I may not spend much time with you." He unrolled a scroll and glanced at it.

"You have been sentenced to stand trial by combat, first with a man, second with a bird, and third with a beast. If you kill the man, that will of course save your life. But if you subdue him without killing him, he will become your slave. If you kill or overcome the bird, you will have the right to ask and be granted a boon by the Emperor. And if you overcome or kill the beast, you will be granted your life and freedom.

"In case you won all three fights, which has never been done, you would go and stand before the golden pavilion in the south, where the Emperor and Empress will be enthroned. You would raise your hand in salute, thus"—raising his right hand with the palm forward—"whereupon the Emperor would give you your freedom."

Examining the scroll once more, the man passed on to the next cage—the one occupied by the bearded white savage.

"What about you, wild one? Can you talk?" he asked.

The bearded man looked at him blankly. Then he began a series of guttural grunts and barks very much like the language of the chimpanzees.

"Ha! So you speak like the hairy ones. Well, no man can understand such noises, so I cannot instruct you."

"I can tell you what he says," volunteered Jan. "He asks what you want. Shall I interpret for you?"

"No use," said the yellow-clad one. "He would not have the intelligence to understand."

AS THE sun approached noon, the attitude of the multitude of spectators in the amphitheater grew tense. Already Samsu, High Priest of Set, had taken his place on the north. He was surrounded by his black-clothed nobles with their ladies, black-armored guards, and black-robed priests.

The seat of honor on the west was occupied by Teta, High Priest of Asar. His impressive title and name were Neter Ka Asar, Teta, Sa Re, or Holy Soul of Isiris, Son of the Sun. Like Samsu, he was a cousin of the Emperor. Surrounding Teta were his white-cloaked nobles and their families, white-armored guards, and white-robed priests.

In the seat of honor on the east side sat Pilatre, High Priestess of Aset. Her title—Neter Urt en Aset, Pilatre, Sat Remeant Divine Great Lady of Isis, Pilatre, Daughter of the Sun. She was Teta's daughter. Pilatre was attired in light blue, and her fierce Amazon guards wore armor lacquered a cerulean shade, while her ladies and her comely vestal virgins wore diaphanous garments of the same azure tint.

The general assembly was a motley jumble of color. Each class dressed according to its trade, profession or occupation, so far as cut and quality of garments went, but with no restrictions as to color, except that no person not definitely allied with one of the four great religious orders might be completely clad in the color of that order. Color combinations of every kind were permissible, and were used to such an extent that a kaleidoscopic effect was produced wherever the people congregated.

Vendors of sweetmeats, nuts, fruits and *chocolatl*, a beverage made from a mixture of chocolate and honey, moved through the crowds, noisily crying their wares. Hawkers of cheap jewelry, gewgaws, trinkets and charms scrambled from tier to tier, shouting the merits of their merchandise. Others sold scrolls of thin papyrus on which a program of the day's events was inscribed in curious hieroglyphic characters.

But the bedlam of sound was suddenly hushed as there came a blare of trumpets from the south. Then, from beneath the stand supporting the golden pavilion, a gold-armored herald dashed out into the arena, mounted on a fierce three-horned steed.

"The Emperor and Empress come!" he cried. "Salute your rulers!"

In an instant, every man, woman and child, from high priest and great noble down to the lowliest slave, bowed the knee. Slowly, majestically, the royal couple came through the arched doorway beside the great golden throne. With quiet dignity they took their seats.

A great cry went up from the crowd:

"To Mena and Nefertre! Life! Strength! Health!"

Having paid this tribute to their exalted rulers, the people resumed their seats.

Surrounded by his gold-armored warriors, his nobles and their ladies, and the yellow-robed priests of Re, Mena watched a small sundial on a pedestal before him. It was the custom to begin the games just as the sun reached the meridian, in order that Re, the Sun God, might look auspiciously down upon them from his great central throne in the heavens.

When the shadow on the dial pointed directly north, Mena raised his scepter. There was a clash of cymbals, a roll of drums, and a blare of trumpets. The games were officially opened.

A mounted herald dashed into the arena and announced:

"His Imperial Majesty, Mena, Son of Re, has commanded that the first event offered for your entertainment today shall be the triple trial for life of the fierce young wild man known as Jan of the Jungle.

"As his life is thrice forfeit, so thrice must he defend it. First was it forfeit to Set, when he blinded the Sebek and escaped from the temple. For this offense he shall do battle with a man. Second, his life is forfeit to the State, as he slew one of her soldiers. For this offense, if he survive the first, he shall do battle with a bird.

"Third, his life is forfeit to the great god Re, because he entered by force the habitation of his High Priest, the Imperial Palace. For this offense, if he survive the other two ordeals, he shall fight a beast. It is the decree of the Emperor that if he survive all three, then will he have earned life and freedom."

STANDING WITH face pressed against the bars of his cell, Jan listened to the announcement of the herald. He saw the riders disappear through the gate beneath the imperial throne. Then the door in the front of his cell was raised. The end of a long pole prodded him in the back, and a gruff voice called, "Out with you!"

With a snarl, Jan turned to seize the pole, but it was snatched away. The attendant who held it behind the bars then dropped the pole and took up a long trident.

Jan saw that sooner or later he must enter the arena. As well do it peacefully as to remain bore and receive wounds that might cripple him. He walked out, and the door clanged into place behind him.

For a moment he stood there undecided where to go or what to do. He had heard it ordained that he must fight a man, yet he was alone in the arena. Perplexed, he started to walk across the white sand. He had reached a point opposite the golden throne of Mena when he heard a clang behind him. Turning, he saw a long-bearded, naked man coming toward him. It was the wild-looking white man who had been confined in the cell next to his.

The man walked forward into the arena, apparently as much at sea as Jan about what he was supposed to do. The youth waited until he came up.

"What do they want us to do?" barked the other in a queer man-ape language.

"To fight, I believe," replied Jan in the same guttural tongue.

At this moment, a gold-armored rider dashed through the gate beneath the throne. Riding up between the two, he threw a heavy knotted club at the feet of each. Then he withdrew.

"Ah, this is better!" exclaimed the bearded man, catching up his club. "We will not have to fight with teeth and nails."

Jan picked up his own club. Then he warily watched his

opponent, who was coming toward him, the club held high over his head, as if he would crush Jan to earth with one blow.

The youth stood his ground. He did not even raise his own weapon. But when the heavy club descended with terrific force, Jan was not there. With cat-like quickness he had leaped lightly to one side. As the bludgeon of his opponent thudded to the sand where he had stood a moment before Jan swung his own weapon.

Had it landed squarely it would have crushed the skull like an eggshell. The blow, however, was only a glancing one. But it struck with enough force to tear the scalp of the bearded man and knock him unconscious. He collapsed in a heap.

It had been ridiculously easy. Jan stood there, leaning on his club, and gazing at his fallen foe. Two armored riders dashed out. One reined his steed to a halt, dismounted, and threw the limp and unconscious body over his mount's back in front of the saddle. The other rider handed Jan a long spear. Then both withdrew.

OVER AT his left, Jan heard the clang of a gate. He looked, and gasped in surprise and awe at sight of the weird and terrifying monstrosity that was trotting toward him on two legs.

It was a bird fully eight feet tall, with a crest on its immense head like that of a kingfisher. Its great, eagle-like beak was large enough and strong enough to pluck off the head of a man at a single snap, and swallow it like a cherry. Its legs, longer and stronger than those of a full-grown horse, terminated in immense, sharp clutching talons.

There had been a picture of this bird of prey standing over its kill in one of Ramona's books. It was called a brontornis, or thunder bird and like many of the other strange creatures he had met within this valley, was supposed to be extinct.

As the immense bird drew near, it cocked its head to one side for a moment as if deciding whether or not Jan would be worth while as a food morsel, considering the risk. It must have made an abrupt decision that he was, for it suddenly spread its short, stubby wings and charged.

Jan extended his spear point, and braced his feet to meet the charge, aiming for the center of the huge, feathery breast.

It was almost upon him, the spear not an inch from its breast, when it suddenly swooped, arched its neck, and snapped downward, seizing the shaft of the weapon in its powerful beak.

Taken completely by surprise, Jan was swept off his feet as the feathered giant gave a quick jerk backward in an effort to pluck the spear from his grasp. He hung on, and the bird, after swinging him far around to the right, suddenly flung its head the other way.

A cry went up from the breathlessly watching crowd as the shaft snapped off and Jan, holding the broken butt, was thrown to the ground.

Dropping the spearhead, the bird leaped for the fallen Jan. Before he could move, it had pinned him beneath one immense foot, its clutching talons embedded in his left, shoulder and arm. Then it threw back its head and uttered a loud ringing cry that momentarily drowned the clamor of the excited onlookers—like a cock crowing over a vanquished rival, but with a voice more nearly resembling that of a lion.

Lying beneath the terrific weight of the feathered giant, with blood gushing from his shoulder and arm where the cruel talons were embedded, Jan struggled desperately to arise, and futilely beat the bird with his slender spear shaft.

Having voiced its cry of victory, the brontornis leisurely bent over to devour its struggling prey. Jan saw the immense head coming down, straight for his face, the powerful hooked beak opened wide—and did the only thing left for him to do. He thrust the splintered end of his spear shaft between the gaping mandible and down the throat.

With a peculiar sound which in a smaller bird might have been a squawk, but coming from this throat was more like a strangled roar, the monster jerked his head up and shook it, trying to dislodge the shaft. But Jan had thrust with all his might, and the splintered end was tightly lodged.

After several futile shakes the bird tried, first with one foot, then the other, to claw the stick from its throat, its prey momentarily forgotten. But when the second foot lifted, Jan was free, and quick to take advantage of his freedom.

Leaping to his feet, he ran to where his heavy club lay. Picking it up, he returned, and swung it with all his strength against the shin of the leg on which the monster was standing. Under the force of that blow the bone shattered like matchwood, and the feathered giant toppled over.

It was up in an instant, however, on its good leg. Jan swung his club again, and the bird slumped to the ground, flapping its useless stubs of wings and squawking thunderously—the spear shaft still protruding from its throat.

Then Jan directed blow after blow at the huge, crested head. Twice that head lolled in the sand as if the monster was quite dead, and twice it was reared again, bruised arid bloody, so tenacious of life was this creature. But the third time it sank, never to rise again.

WHILE THE onlookers roared their approval, Jan threw down his club and walked over before the golden throne. It was the first time he had had a good look at the Emperor and Empress; and he was surprised. Somehow he had expected Mena to be old and hideous like the High Priest, Samsu. He was astonished, therefore, to see a handsome, smooth-shaved, athletic-looking man, not yet forty. His wife, Nefertre, was not only quite young-looking, but beautiful. She reminded Jan of Ramona, as if she might indeed have been an elder sister or her mother.

The Emperor stood up.

"You have earned a reward, Jan of the jungle," he said, not unkindly. "Name it."

"I ask that the prisoner, Prince Koh of Temukan, be freed and sent back unharmed to his father with a suitable escort," said Jan.

The Emperor looked astonished.

"Prince Koh has been condemned to the games," he said. "He is to appear in the next event. I cannot—"

He did not finish his sentence, for the Empress had suddenly reached over, laid her hand on his arm, and said something to him in a low voice. Jan could not hear what she said, but he surmised that she was interceding for him, as she gave him a little friendly smile. At first Mena shook his head firmly, but gradually, as his beautiful wife talked to him he seemed to relent.

"Very well, Jan of the jungle," he said. "Your request is granted." He turned to the master of ceremonies. "Go on with the next event."

Through one of the numerous gates beneath the tiers of seats lumbered a great hairy beast with long, curling tusks. A uniformed trainer rode on its neck, and an attendant followed, carrying a sharp, three-pronged hook at the end of a heavy chain, trailing from a collar around the great beast's neck.

At first Jan thought he was going to have to fight this monster, a mighty bull mastodon, but he breathed easier when it passed him unnoticed, and stopped near the carcass of the bird. The man holding the hook jabbed a prong into the feathery body, the trainer shouted a command, and the great prehistoric beast of burden moved away, dragging the remains of the thunder bird with ease.

Scarcely had the carcass of the feathered giant disappeared when a gold-armored rider galloped out of the gate beneath the throne. He handed Jan a longbow, a quiver of arrows, and a short sword with scabbard and belt. Jan buckled the sword belt around his waist and slung the quiver by its strap beneath his left arm so the feathered ends of the arrows could be reached quickly, and wondered what manner of monster he was doomed to fight this time.

He had not long to wait, for a gate clanged over at his right, and there stalked into the arena the most powerful and ferocious of beats—a giant saber-toothed tiger.

CHAPTER XXV

RAKING CLAWS

STANDING IN THE center of the arena, Jan felt quite small and insignificant in the presence of the mighty carnivore that was stalking majestically toward him. He realized that the chances were all against him, jungle champion though he was, for winning a battle with a saber-toothed tiger. He was in greater danger than he had ever been before.

He fitted an arrow to the bowstring and waited. A shaft launched from a distance would only infuriate the brute and hasten its charge. But should the cat continue its slow, majestic pace, he might be able to send an arrow through an eye into the brain from a distance of fifty feet or so.

No sound came from the myriad onlookers in the seats above. They were watching silently, breathlessly, to see how the contestant would play this extremely dangerous game. It promised almost certain death.

Seated on the lowest tier before the throne were two archers, whose duty it was to see that animals which did not show a fighting spirit in the arena were goaded to greater ferocity. For this purpose they had longbows, and arrows with barbed heads, backed by cross pieces that prevented their piercing beyond a depth of two inches. A few of these barbed arrows clinging to its sides and flank usually put any beast in a fighting humor.

One of the archers, observing that the advancing tiger did not appear any more ferocious than a house cat confronted by a dish of milk, fitted a barbed arrow to the string, and nudged his companion.

"The youth is waiting for a close, careful shot," he said, "hoping it will be deadly. Watch me spoil his plans." He drew the arrow back to his ear, took deliberate aim, and let fly.

At the twang of the bowstring the feline looked up curiously. Then, as the cruel barb suddenly stung its shoulder, it gave vent to a roar of rage and charged, not at Jan in the center of the arena, but straight for the archer who had launched the arrow.

It was fully fifteen feet from the floor of the arena to the lowest tier, but the tiger made it in a single graceful leap. Before the astonished and horrified archer could draw his sword, the great cat was upon him. A single crunch of the powerful jaws crushed his head to bloody pulp.

All this took place in a few seconds, but during that brief time Jan had not been idle. As the great beast launched itself into the air, he sent an arrow into its side. By the time it had slain the archer he had sent a second arrow after the first.

Then he saw the monster knocking armored soldiers right and left with sledge-hammer blows from its powerful front paws as it made straight for the golden throne. There were cries of horror from the spectators—shrieks of terror from the ladies who sat with the nobles on each side of the throne.

The Emperor stood up and drew his sword. The Empress turned deathly pale, but stood her ground. There was but a thin line of soldiers between the monster and the throne.

Jan cared nothing for the archers and the soldiers. He cared nothing for the fate of the Emperor. All these were his enemies. But the Empress had smiled at him, with a smile that reminded him of Ramona. And she had interceded with her husband for him. She was his friend; and she was in deadly peril.

Dropping his bow, Jan sprinted for the gateway beneath the throne. Reaching it, he leaped upward, grasped the ornamental rim of the arch above it, and drew himself up. Just above the arch hung the imperial banner of Satmu, draped over the wall. Jan seized a golden tassel, pulled himself up, and grasping the edge of the banner, clambered upward.

Flinging an arm over the rim of the wall, he swung his body across. Then he whipped out his shortsword and charged over the fallen warriors in the wake of the flailing, roaring tiger.

BETWEEN THE throne and the charging fury there remained but one man. He was Telapu, son of Samsu, Captain of the Imperial Guard and Crown Warrior. Despite his armor and his longsword, Telapu could not bring himself to face the monster that had knocked his men about like ninepins. With a shriek of terror, he turned and ran, leaving the Emperor and Empress to face the beast unguarded.

It was at this moment that Jan came up behind the tiger. With a mighty leap he alighted on the shaggy back, and grasping the loose skin of the neck, thrust his shortsword in to the hilt just beneath the shoulder blade.

Sounding a frightful roar, the great cat turned to seize its foe. But it toppled backward. Jan and the tiger rolled together to the lowest tier, where they brought up against the edge of the wall with terrific force.

As they lay there motionless, apparently locked in a death embrace, it was the Emperor who first dashed down the steps to Jan's aid. Lifting a heavy paw which lay across Jan's chest, he dragged his limp body away from that of his terrible foe.

Then he shouted for the royal physician and attendants. The Empress, who had hurried after him, bent over the youth and laid her hand over his heart.

"May Re be praised!" she exclaimed. "He lives! You must see that he is fittingly rewarded for this brave deed, my lord."

"Such reward as is in our power to confer shall be his," replied the Emperor. Then he uttered a sudden exclamation of surprise as he noticed the emblem tattooed in the palm of Jan's right hand. "Look! The sacred lotus! This is no common savage, but a prince of the blood imperial! It accounts for his extraordinary bravery."

"You forget, my lord," said Nefertre, "that Telapu is also of the blood imperial. Does this, then, account for his cowardice?"

"It's a different strain," replied Mena; "a throw-back, which by Heru and Anpu I'll weed from my ranks!... But here's the doctor."

JAN WAKENED in a soft bed beneath yellow silken coverlets in which were embroidered the imperial coat of arms of Satmu. His head, shoulder and arm were neatly bandaged, and his tattered garments of jaguar skin had been replaced with a silken sleeping wrap.

When he sat up and saw the magnificence of the bedchamber, he thought at first that he had arrived in that beautiful place called heaven, which Ramona had described. But his head swam dizzily, and he subsided to the pillow once more. He recalled rolling down the tiers of the amphitheater in the dying clutch of the tiger, and the conviction, as his head struck the wall, that his time had come to sleep the long sleep.

But there was a saffron-skinned Temukanese slave standing at the foot of his bed. Had this slave also gone to heaven?

"Where are we?" he asked.

"In the Imperial Palace, highness," replied the slave respectfully.

"Where is Prince Koh of Temukan?" asked Jan.

"He awaits the permission of the royal physician to visit your highness, before beginning his journey."

"Tell the royal physician I want to see the prince now," said Jan.

The slave bowed low and withdrew. In a few moments he returned with a tall, dignified man, whose upper lip and jowls were shaven, but whose chin was adorned with a short gray beard, rectangular in shape and plaited with fine gold threads.

"I am Usephais, the doctor, highness," he said. "So you would entertain visitors? It must be that you are recovering rapidly. Let us see."

He unwound Jan's bandages, one by one, and examined his wounds. Then he listened to his heart, and felt his brow for fever.

"Head ache?" he asked.

"Not much," replied Jan, "but it swims when I sit up."

"I know. That will pass. Here drink this."

He dissolved a powder in a glass of wine and held it to the patient's lips.

Jan drank, and immediately felt a grateful glow suffusing him.

"We'll have you up and around in a day or two," said Usephais, "but for the present you must stay in bed. You may see your friend, however."

He withdrew, and within a short time, Prince Koh was kneeling at the bedside.

"I don't know how to thank you," he said, gripping Jan's hand. "Since your brilliant defense of their majesties, yesterday, I've been treated as a visiting prince rather than a captured slave. And I'm to leave for my native kingdom of Temukan today with an escort."

Some time later Jan was visited by the Emperor and Empress. Because of his ignorance of human customs or the formality of courts, he had no idea of the honor bestowed upon him by such a visit, but he flushed under their enthusiastic praise of his valor, and something within him that had always longed for the care and love of a real human mother responded to the maternal ministrations of the beautiful Nefertre, who could talk to him so soothingly, and whose cool, soft hand upon his brow seemed to bestow a healing benediction.

BY ORDER of the royal physician, he was kept in his apartments for three days. On the fourth he was summoned to the imperial audience chamber.

The page who brought the summons was followed by a half dozen slaves, who bore quilted silken garments, gold-plated armor and weapons. While the Emperor's messenger waited, the slaves quickly dressed Jan in the silken garments, fastened his armor on him, and belted his sword and dagger about his waist. Then he followed the page to the throne room.

Mena was seated on a jewel-studded golden throne, on a dais at one end of the room. Above the back of the throne, a brilliantly polished golden globe, representing the sun, was supported by three images: a blue one of Aset, cut from lapis lazuli; a white one of Asar, carved from alabaster; and a black one of Set, sculptured from polished jet.

Standing at each side of the throne were the leading nobles officials and dignitaries of the realm, including the High Priest of Asar and that of Set, and the High Priestess of Aset.

As Jan and the page entered the room, a major-domo announced:

"His Royal Highness Prince Jan."

Then the page conducted him to the foot of the throne, while every voice was hushed, and every eye was turned upon him.

The Emperor stood up to receive him, an unusual honor, and made public acknowledgment of the crown's indebtedness to him for his act of heroism at the games.

Then the monarch resumed his seat and glanced over to the left where Samsu High Priest of Set, stood with a little group of his black-clad followers.

"I believe you have a petition, Samsu," he said.

"I have, your majesty," replied the High Priest. "The savage who stands before your throne blinded the holy Sebek. I ask that he be given into my hands, that he may be punished for this sacrilege."

"He has already stood trial by combat on that score," replied Mena. "The incident is closed."

"In the name of the great god Set I demand justice!" said Samsu his skull-like face working.

"Well, then, justice you shall have," said Mena. "Telapu!"

Standing at the right of the throne, Samsu's craven son turned deathly pale, and his knees quaked violently when he suddenly heard his name spoken by the Emperor. Nothing had been said to him about his display of cowardice at the games and he was beginning to believe that on account of the influence of his father, the matter had been overlooked.

"Yes, your majesty," he replied, his voice quavering.

"Your services as Captain of the Imperial Guard are no longer required. The title of Crown Warrior is yours no longer. I return you to your father and to the ranks of the black ones. Go!"

The eyes of Samsu flashed an angry green. Here was a decided setback to his ambition. For Mena had no heir, and he had hoped to place his son in line for succession to the throne of Satmu. But he dared not utter a word of protest. As Telapu, pale and tearful, stumbled over to "where he stood, he kept his head bowed.

"Prince Jan," said Mena rising once more. "In the presence of these witnesses, I name you Crown Warrior and Captain of the Imperial Guard."

He raised his hand dismissing the court.

Samsu, his face plainly showing his hate and envy, departed with his disgraced son and his black-clad followers, while the other courtiers crowded around Jan to congratulate him.

CHAPTER XXVI

THE VANQUISHED

SHORTLY AFTER JAN returned to his quarters a page entered and bowed before him.

"Your highness's slave by combat awaits leave to come into your presence," he said.

"My slave by combat? What do you mean?"

"It is the one your highness overcame in the arena. Shall I send him in?"

"Yes."

A moment later a slender, stately individual, whose iron-gray beard was trimmed to a sharp point, and whose neat court attire and well-groomed person proclaimed his gentility, walked into the apartment. Wrapped around his head was a clean white bandage. Jan, who had expected to see the hairy wild man he had vanquished at the games, was astounded. Yet on close scrutiny, there seemed to be a slight resemblance between this man and the one he had stunned with his club.

"Who are you?" asked Jan.

"I am Sir Henry Westgate of the outer world," replied the man, accenting his Satmuan speech as if unfamiliar with its use yet understanding it. "I have been told you came here from the outer world. What language did you speak there?"

"English," replied Jan. "Also a few Indian and Spanish words.

"I am English," said Sir Henry. "These people tell me I become your slave since you vanquished me in the arena. I do not remember fighting you. Can you tell me about it?"

Jan told him how he had first seen him in a cage next to his beneath the seats of the amphitheater and of the fights that followed.

When he had finished, the Englishman said:

"This is terrible tragic! I must have lost my memory for years. No doubt that blow in the arena restored it. They tell me I was captured, quite naked, with a band of hairy men, who were brought in for the games.

"I was exploring the jungle, looking for a way to this very city, the existence of which I suspected. As I wandered through the wilds I lost many members of my expedition. Some fell prey to wild beasts, some to the long arrows and poisonous darts of the savages, and some to the fever. Finally, when I was reduced to but four followers, I left camp one morning on a lone trip of exploration. After traveling several miles I came to a tall cliff. I am a trained climber, and had brought a rope. After hours of effort I succeeded in reaching the top of that cliff, and found that I was on the top of a long ridge about five hundred feet wide, enclosing a vast green valley. With my field glasses I made out what looked like a good-sized city about fifteen miles from where I stood. I was sure this was the city for which I had been searching.

"There was a shelf about fifty feet below, and beneath this a number of other shelves. I had a sixty-foot rope, and this I made fast about the base of a stunted tree that grew on the cliff top. Then I let myself down over the cliff. I reached the first shelf without mishap, and the second.

"As I was descending to the third I heard shouts below me— sounds manlike and yet beast-like. Looking down; I saw a score of primitive beast-men, bearded, whose bodies were covered with hair. They began to hurl sticks and stones up at me. I tried to scramble back up on the shelf, but a missile struck the side of my head, and all went black.

"I remember nothing more that happened until I returned to consciousness here in the palace three days ago. I know only that years must have passed, because my hair and beard grew so long and turned so gray."

"And now you wish to go back to the outer world?" asked Jan.

No. I prefer to remain here in Satmu, to study its people. It is a privilege for which I would give many years of my life."

"Then do so," said Jan. "If the fact that I knocked you unconscious made you my slave, you are free from now on," and extended his hand, as he had seen white men do. The English scientist took it gratefully.

AS THE days passed, lengthened into weeks and months, Jan grew tired of the luxury and splendor of his life in the palace, and longed for the simplicity and freedom of his former jungle life. He often thought of Ramona, and wished that he could revisit the plantation to see if she had returned from her journey. But he had come to Satmu by such a devious way that he had no idea where to look for the underground passageway through which he had entered the valley.

Mena had given orders that he be instructed in reading and writing, in the arts and sciences, and in the use of aims. He progressed rapidly with his studies, and still more rapidly in the use of weapons, which he took to as naturally as a duck to water, thanks to his jungle-trained skill and coordination. In a few months he could fence as well as his master. The best archer in the army could not send an arrow or hurl a javelin straighter or farther than he.

As for riding the fierce three-horned steeds, he had a way with the brutes that even the most experienced riders could not duplicate.

Having learned to ride and to fence, he was taught tilting, a sport in which long lances and shields were used by the two rivals in each match. In the practice bouts, blunt lances were used, the object being to unseat an opponent. But in jousting matches and duels, lances with needle-sharp points were employed.

He often went on hunting excursions, sometimes with small parties, and sometimes, when the Emperor went, with large forces of hunters. The valley abounded in big game, and the hunters riding their swift, three-horned steeds usually found excellent sport. Following the hunters came the mastodons with their drivers and attendants. The attendants cleaned and cut up the game, and loaded it on the backs of the huge woolly pachyderms, to be conveyed back to Satmu.

One day when Jan was out with a small party of hunters, he sighted a giant ground sloth some distance away, squatting on its haunches and eating the leaves of a tree. The party had been following a herd of deer, but when Jan saw this immense creature, he left the others and hurried his mount toward it.

He had not gone far when the mylodon must have decided that the leaves were more luscious farther on, and lumbered away with considerable speed, for despite its awkwardness and immense bulk it could travel quite swiftly. Soon it was leading Jan across a stretch of marsh land, dotted with little clumps of trees. And here the sloth made swifter progress than the pursuing triceratops, as its broad pads were better adapted to this travel than those of Jan's steed.

It took more than two hours to cross the marsh. By this time, Jan had lost sight of his quarry. But the trail was plain enough, and he urged his mount along this at top speed. Soon he emerged from the tree-sprinkled country onto a broad grassy plain. Less than a half mile away he saw the mylodon.

Here, with the advantage all in favor of the triceratops, he gained rapidly on the monster. As he came up behind it, it turned, and rearing itself on its thick tail and sturdy hind legs, awaited his coming.

Jan couched his long lance and charged. He had aimed for the left breast, and the lace point struck and entered the target unswervingly. With a terrible screaming roar, the mylodon swung its two powerful forefeet in retaliation. An immense paw struck Jan with a terrific impact, and sent him rolling in the

tall grass fully twenty feet away from his saddle. For a moment
he lay there, half stunned.

The mylodon, apparently mortally wounded, was bellowing,
moaning and threshing about in the grass. But the triceratops,
having lost its rider, was galloping back toward Satmu by the
way it had come, as fast as its stout legs would carry it.

Jan shouted to his runaway steed at the top of his voice, but
with no effect.

HAD HE been a city-bred man, confronted by the prospect
of being left alone in this wilderness, Jan might have sunk to
the utmost depths of despair. But to this man of the jungle
being alone in the wilds was a pleasure. It was easy for him to
slip back into the old ways.

He waited until the great sloth lay still. Then, with his keen
dagger, he carved a steak from the rump and ate until his hunger
was satisfied. Nor did he neglect carving off another piece and
wrapping it in a strip of tough hide as a provision against future
needs.

After he had eaten, Jan was thirsty, and the breeze from the
south carried the scent of water. He accordingly set out in that
direction. As he did so, there came to him the howling of a
hyaenodon that had scented the kill, answered by a score of
canine throats from all directions.

A half hour's walk brought him to the bank of a river that
meandered between low, willow-fringed banks. After he had
drunk his fill, he looked downstream, and noticed that there
was something strangely familiar about the locality in which
he found himself. An unbroken line of tall, perpendicular cliffs
confronted him, and the river disappeared into the face of one
of these, not two miles from where he stood. On the left bank
of the stream stood the temple ruins and the great stone images
that he had seen when he first entered the valley.

Here, then, was the lost passageway! The gateway to his
beloved jungle, and perhaps to that beautiful creature beyond

the jungle who had gone on a long journey, but who had promised she would return and wait for him.

Hungry for a sight of his jungle once more, and thrilled at the prospect of finding Ramona, Jan lost no time in getting to the temple ruins. As it was impossible for him to swim weighted down with his armor and weapons, he made a light raft from pieces of driftwood bound together with strands of twisted grass. Then he stripped, and after piling his clothing, armor and weapons on the raft, pushed out into the stream.

Inside the cavern, he dragged his craft up on the bank, and dressed once more. Then he followed the dark passageway to the opening beneath the falls, descended the cliff face, plunged through the sheet of falling water and waded ashore.

A glance upward revealed that his tree house was still there. Joyously climbing the bank, he made for the base of the great tree that had been his home for so long.

But he came to a sudden halt, as two rifles cracked almost in unison. At the impact of the two projectiles, Jan spun halfway round, then fell.

CHAPTER XXVII

A FIGHTING VICTIM

AS JAN FELL to the ground, Dr. Bracken's two Indian watchers their rifles still smoking, leaped from their hiding place and ran toward him with exultant shouts.

But much to their surprise and consternation, the victim got to his feet just as they reached him. His sword leaped from its sheath. One savage was pierced before he could recover from his astonishment. The other quickly turned and fled into the jungle.

Jerking his blade free of the sagging body, Jan hurried after the running Indian. But the weight of his armor impeded him. Whipping bow and arrow from the quiver at his back, he sent a steel-tipped shaft after his fleeing assailant.

It struck the Indian in the back of the neck and passed through, inflicting a mortal wound. By the time Jan came up beside him, he was dead.

Having made sure that the savage was sleeping the long sleep, Jan returned to the base of the tree. Here, he curiously examined the armor covering his left shoulder, where the two projectiles had struck. It was dented in two places, but not broken through. He saw one of the projectiles lying nearby—a crumpled hollow cylinder with liquid dripping from it, and the broken stub of a needle on one end.

Before proceeding on into the jungle, Jan decided to inspect the tree house. But in order to climb, he was forced to remove his metal shoes and gauntlets. These he slung by straps around his neck. Then he made the ascent.

Most of the articles in the tree house seemed to be as he had left them, except that the *machetes* and other iron weapons had rusted. The roof had several holes in it where parts of the thatch had blown away, and the floor was littered with leaves and bits of grass that had fallen from the roof.

Although his armor had saved him from the hypodermic bullets of the two Indians, Jan was beginning to grow quite tired of it. He was as proud of it as is any high school boy with a new raccoon coat, and pride dictated that he should keep it on, that Ramona might witness its splendor.

But he could not run with it on, nor swing through the trees, hence his trip to the Suarez plantation would be slowed down. He decided to leave it in the tree house.

With the aid of his dagger and a rawhide thong, he quickly fashioned himself a garment from one of his jaguar hides. Then he removed his armor and silken garments, piled them on the floor, and covered them with another hide. He also decided to leave his sword, as it might impede his movements, and take with him only his bow and arrows and his dagger.

As he descended the tree and plunged into the jungle, he exulted in the feeling of freedom induced by his change of costume. It was good to feel the warm air blowing on his bare head and naked limbs. And the soft leaf mold caressed the soles of his feet, which for months had been shod with metal. This jungle, to him, was home.

Night found him many miles from his tree house, comfortably curled in a crotch high above the ground, here the evening breeze, gently swaying the tree-tops, softly lulled him to sleep.

HE ROSE with the sun, and finding the meat he had brought with him a bit too high for palatability, he flung it away and shot a peccary. Having breakfasted, he set off once more toward the north.

It was late afternoon of the third day when he reached the

ceiba tree under the roots of which he had slept during those days which had passed all too swiftly before Ramona's departure for the United States.

He was about to peer into his former retreat when he suddenly heard a girl scream, as if in deadly terror. He heard several more muffled cries. Then all was still as before. The sound had come from far over to his right. And the voice was undoubtedly that of Ramona. Just once before had he heard her utter such a scream—on that eventful day when he had stepped between her and the charging puma.

With the swiftness of a leaping deer, he bounded off in the direction from which the sounds had come.

It was some time before Jan reached the spot from which the cries had come. But once there, his jungle-trained eyes instantly read the story of the girl's futile struggle with two Indians. From this point, the trail they had taken was as plain to Jan as is a concrete pavement to a motorist: He bad not gone far before he again heard the voice of Ramona, mingled with the gruff tones and coarse laughter of a man.

A moment more, and he emerged into a small clearing just in time to see the girl being dragged into the dark interior of a hut by some invisible person.

With an involuntary snarl, he bounded across the clearing and entered the hut. As he had plunged from the bright sunlight into semi-darkness, there was an instant when he could see nothing. During that instant, a pistol blazed at him from beside a shadowy bulk that loomed in the darkness, and a sharp pain seared his side.

Jan launched himself at that shadowy form. One hand sought and found the wrist that held the pistol. The other gripped a sinewy throat. The pistol roared again, so close that the powder burned his shoulder. Jan suddenly bent and seized the gun wrist in his teeth. There was a lurid Spanish curse, and the weapon thudded to the clay floor.

Although Jan was far stronger than the average man, his

Jan, fully armored once more, was riding beside
the emperor on his monstrous steed.

advantage was offset by the fact that his opponent knew, and
did not hesitate to employ, almost every trick of wrestling and
boxing, as well as many which are barred both on the mat and
in the ring.

Striking, biting, clutching, clawing, gouging, and kicking,
they fought there in the semi-darkness with the ferocity of
jungle beasts. Presently, locked in a vise-like clinch, they swayed
and fell to the floor. Rolling over and over, they crashed through
the flimsy wall of the hut and out into the sunlight. And it was
there, when his eyes became adjusted to the change of light,
that Jan recognized Santos, his old enemy.

The sight added fuel to the flames of his anger—gave a new
impetus to his fast-waning strength. Santos bad clamped on
an arm-lock that would have broken the bones of one less
mightily thewed. But his eyes caught the glitter of Jan's jeweled
dagger hilt which the youth had completely forgotten in this
primitive struggle with nature's weapons.

The captain had nearly reached the limit of his endurance:
If he could get that dagger he might end the contest in his favor

with a single, well-placed thrust. But he could not reach for it
without giving up the advantage which the arm-lock gave him,
as this kept both his hands occupied. He must therefore act
with lightning swiftness.

He increased the pressure on Jan's arm, then suddenly let go
and, straightening up, grabbed for the dagger. Jan had been
resisting the hold by curving the arm downward. As the captain
released it, his hand came in contact with a smooth, round
stone, half embedded in the soft clay.

With a grunt of triumph, Santos jerked the dagger from its
sheath and raised it aloft. But at this instant, Jan swung the
stone, catching him between the eyes. At the impact of that
terrific blow, the dagger dropped from Santos's nerveless fingers,
and he slumped forward.

FLINGING THE limp body of his enemy from him, Jan
picked up his dagger, sheathed it, and hurried into the hut.
There on the floor, in a little crumpled heap, lay Ramona, as
limp and apparently as lifeless as the captain.

Tenderly, Jan picked her up and carried her out into the
sunlight. So far as he could see, there were no marks of violence
on her other than the red lines where the rope had chafed her
wrists.

A great fear entered his heart. Perhaps he had arrived too
late, after all. Perhaps the weapon which had creased his ribs
and burned his shoulder had slain her in some mysterious
manner, and she was sleeping the long sleep.

But in a moment Ramona, who had fainted, opened her eyes.
Weakly she flung an arm around his neck, snuggled more closely
against his shoulder.

"I waited so long for you, Jan," she murmured. "I thought
you would never come."

As he stood there holding her in his arms and looking down
into her great dark eyes, Jan saw a light in them that kindled
the smoldering flame in his bosom and sent the blood coursing

madly through his strong young body. Unconsciously he held her tighter. Slowly he bent over her lips.

Once before in her life she had kissed him. The farewell of a child, a playmate. That kiss he would always remember. But in the interval of separation, Nature and the longing each had felt for the other, had wrought a wondrous change. Now the fires of their youthful love flamed as their lips met.

Her arm tightened around his neck, stole up to caress his tangle of auburn curls.

"I love you, Ramona," he murmured.

"Jan! Take me away with you! Don't ever leave me again!"

With Ramona still in his arms Jan strode off into the jungle, her slight weight as nothing to him.

"Oh, Jan! What have I said? What have we done? Put me down! Please!"

Puzzled, he stood her on her feet.

"You must take me home, Jan. I didn't mean what I said."

"You mean you don't want to come with me?"

"I must hurry home. I don't know what made me say what I did. My people will be worried frantic about me. And tomorrow I leave again, for school."

Hearing that, Jan felt crushed.

"All right," he said soberly, "I'll take you home."

They had not taken more than a dozen steps in the direction of the hacienda, when there came to them the sounds of men's voices, and a trampling and crashing through the undergrowth.

CHAPTER XXVIII

JUNGLE MAN-HUNT

AT SOME DISTANCE from his base camp, Dr. Bracken, with several of his Indians, was tramping through the jungle when the two who had abducted Ramona dashed breathlessly out into the trail, their expressions plainly showing their excitement.

The doctor stopped.

"What the devil is the matter?" he demanded. "Where are you two going?"

"El Diablo kill captain!" panted one of them.

Dr. Bracken knew that by. "El Diablo" they referred to Jan.

"Where is he? Quick!"

"Over at *malocca!* Captain build hut, steal *señorita* from hacienda! Diablo come! Kill captain!"

"Served him right, the dirty double-crosser!" snarled the doctor. "But come! Show me where! We'll catch this Diablo now, for sure." He shouted an order to the other Indians standing along the trail. "Quick, men—follow me!" Then he dashed off with the two guides.

"Why didn't you catch El Diablo?" he demanded, as they raced along.

"Got no rifles," grunted one. "Can't catch without the rifles."

"Afraid of him, eh? You stood there and let him kill your captain."

"No. Captain already dead. He send us away. We hear shots.

Go back. Captain on ground. El Diablo going into hut. We run hunt for you."

But before they got to the *malocca* the doctor suddenly saw a shaft of sunlight flash on a tousled mass of auburn curls, a light skin, and a spotted garment of jaguar hide. He snapped his rifle to his shoulder and fired.

JAN HEARD the sound of men coming through the jungle toward them. He stopped and looked about him while Ramona went ahead. At that instant a rifle cracked, and a bullet, striking a twig beside him went whining on its way. Crouching low, he hurried to where the girl stood waiting for him.

"Come!" he said to Ramona. "They are after us. They are too many for us to fight. We must run."

It took every ounce of jungle cunning Jan possessed to elude the doctor and his savage pack, as he piloted Ramona through the tangled vegetation. He was forced to zigzag, and at times to double in his tracks, but always his course led him nearer and nearer to the hacienda. And always the pack was close at his heels.

Presently, after some two hours of running and dodging, they emerged in the don's grove of young rubber trees. The sound of the hunters crashing through the jungle grew louder behind them.

Jan stopped.

"Good-bye," he said. "Run to the house! Hurry! I'll lead them another way."

"But, Jan—There is something I—that is—your father and mother—"

"Hurry!" he snapped. "They are almost here." Then he swarmed up a thick liana, swung onto a limb, and disappeared in the dense tangle of foliage.

Ramona stood there uncertainly for a moment, looking at the spot where he had vanished. But the sound of the running savages, now only a few hundred feet away, recalled her to her peril, and she turned and ran breathlessly to the patio.

After Jan turned back into the jungle, climbing from tree to tree, it was not long before he saw his pursuers coming toward him. And in their midst was a figure that aroused in him all the pent-up hatred that years of abuse had engendered—Dr. Bracken.

His intention had been to wait until the man-hunters had passed beneath him, then shout to attract their attention and lead them in the other direction. But that was before he knew that his ancient enemy led the party.

From the Satmuan quiver at his back he drew bow and arrow. Then he took deliberate aim at the bearded figure, and let fly. Pierced through the chest, the doctor uttered a choking cry and collapsed. At the twang of his bow, the Indians stopped, peering ahead of them to see whence it had come. But they did not think to look upward.

There was a second twang, and one of the Indians pitched forward on his face, shot through the heart. The others turned and fled, scattering in all directions, but two more of their number fell before they were out of bow-shot.

Jan returned his bow to the quiver and swung forward through the branches. He paused, directly above his fallen enemy. The doctor's white, upturned features were motionless. His eyes were closed.

For a moment, Jan stared down at the hated face. Then he went onward into the depths of the jungle. When he had traveled for a considerable distance, he sighted a curassow and remembered that he had not eaten for some time. The bird fell before his arrow, and he descended to the ground. With his keen dagger for a carving knife, Jan sat down to his savage feast.

Having eaten, he went to the river for a drink of water. Then darkness set in, and he climbed a tree for the night.

MORNING FOUND him in a quandary as to where to go or what to do. Ramona's actions' had both puzzled and piqued him. Why, he wondered, had she begged him with one breath to take her away, and with the next, insisted that he take her back to her people? Like many an older and more experienced male, Jan came to the conclusion that the feminine mind was baffling.

She had said she was going away. So he finally decided that he would go and try to see her before she left—perhaps persuade her to come with him. Failing in this, he would return to Satmu and try to forget her. He accordingly set off along the river bank.

When he reached the hacienda, Jan proceeded with caution. He heard much talking, then a loud cheer, and cries of *"Adios!"*

Hurrying forward, he peered through the bushes. Just ahead of him was the dock, and on it many people were standing. There were Indians, half-breeds and white people; men, women and children. They were waving farewell to a fleet of canoes that was heading down the river. In the foremost canoe rode Ramona.

Jan's heart sank. He felt very lonely and forsaken. For some time he watched the people on the dock. He noticed, among the others, a woman whose hair was the precise color of his own. He thought her very beautiful. Her sweet face, with its big, wistful eyes, attracted him unaccountably. She was clinging to the arm of a tall, dark-haired, sun-bronzed man he had not seen before. Together with the don and doña, they walked to the house.

Jan turned away, heavy-hearted. Leisurely, he made his way back to his tree house, hunting as he traveled, and taking five days. He approached it cautiously, fearful of ambush. But there was no one about. The skeletons of the two Indians he had slain lay where they had fallen, picked clean by jungle scavengers.

Somehow the place did not seem so alluring to him as he had imagined it would when in Satmu. Here was nothing but desolation and loneliness. With Ramona gone, it was unbearable. Every man he met was his enemy.

In Satmu he had many friends—good comrades with whom he could joust, fence or hunt. The hidden valley now attracted

him as much as the jungle had drawn him before. He decided
to return to Satmu. It would be the place to try to forget—to
shape his life anew.

Jan found his armor, clothing and sword lying where he had
left them. Descending to the ground, he carried them up under
the falls, climbed to the chamber above, and made his way to
where he had left his raft. Here he stripped to the skin, leaving
his jaguar-hide garment in the cave and piling everything else
on his narrow raft.

Pushing off, he swam out into the channel. Soon he emerged
into the bright daylight of the hidden valley He was swimming
for the side on which the temple ruins stood when something
splashed in the water quite near him. Then he heard much
splashing from the direction of the opposite bank.

Turning, he saw a large band of hairy men, some standing
on the bank hurling sticks and stones at him, others plunging
into the water and swimming toward him.

With missiles splashing about him he pivoted and tried to
drag his narrow raft swiftly to the other bank. But a large stone
struck the edge of the unstable craft tilting it and spilling his
armor and weapons, all of which sank immediately.

Abandoning the now useless raft, he quickly swam out of
range of the missiles and made the shore.

Stark naked, he ran up the bank with the water dripping
from his glistening body. Then he sprinted along the broken,
weed-grown avenue lined by the giant stone images, straight
for the temple ruins.

Close behind him came a howling mob of hairy, wild men,
brandishing clubs and hurling such bits of stone as they could
catch up while running.

CHAPTER XXIX

THE GRAVEN ARROW

WHEN RAMONA DASHED into the patio after her rescue by Jan, she found no one there. She passed on through the big house, and found it empty and deserted. But in front of the house she heard excited voices. As she burst out onto the veranda she saw most of the plantation personnel assembled on the river front. Harry Trevor and Don Fernando, having divided their available forces, were each ready to lead a search party into the jungle.

Her old duenna, Señora Soledade, was weeping hysterically, while Georgia Trevor and the doña tried to quiet her. Ramona ran up to where the three women stood, and all attempted to embrace her at once.

As soon as they had ascertained that she was unharmed, everybody, it seemed, was asking her questions at one time.

She told them of her kidnaping by Santos, her rescue by Jan, and the pursuit by Santos's Indians, which she had just escaped at the edge of the clearing.

Within a short time the two parties that had been organized to hunt for her had united, and forming a long line started out to look for Jan.

Harry Trevor was forcing his way through the dense undergrowth when he heard a shout far over at his left. This was followed by excited talking. Hurrying over, he saw Don Fernando and two of his plantation hands bending over a man lying on the ground. As he came closer he saw that the man was Dr. Bracken. The feathered shaft of an arrow protruded from his chest. The don had opened the man's bloodstained shirt front, and was listening for heartbeats:

"Is he dead?" asked Trevor, coming up beside him.

"His heart still beats," replied the don. "He may pull through. The arrow seems to have pierced the upper right lobe of his lung."

"Better get that arrow out of him, hadn't we?" suggested Trevor.

"Have to pack the wound when we do," replied Don Fernando, "or he may bleed to death. We'll take him to the house just as he is."

Under the don's directions a litter was quickly made from two saplings with branches placed across them. On this the doctor was gently laid, and carried to the hacienda. Then a canoe was dispatched for Padre Luis, a missionary priest living with a tribe of Indians down the river. He was reputed to have great medical skill.

SOME HOURS later the *padre* arrived. After extracting the arrow and dressing the wound, he announced that if no infection set in, the patient would probably recover. When he left the sick room, he took along the two pieces of the arrow he had removed. Together with the don and Trevor, he entered the library.

"A strange arrow for these parts, *señores*," he said. "No Indian workmanship there. The head is of tempered, polished steel. The band behind it is pure gold. Those hieroglyphics on the band, besides, are not Indian writing."

He handed the pieces to Don Fernando.

"Why!" exclaimed the don. "They look like the picture writing on the basket!"

"Basket?" asked the *padre*.

"A strange basket I found floating down the river some years ago," replied the don, who in his excitement at sight of the characters had almost betrayed the family secret. "But wait. I have a code. Sir Henry Westgate, an archaeologist who passed through here a number of years ago, left it with me."

He took a bulky manuscript, yellow with age, from a desk drawer, and thumbed through it. Presently he stopped, and with pad and pencil noted the characters on the gold band and compared them with those on the manuscript page. Presently he read:

" 'Warrior of the Prince, Tchan, Son of the Sun.'

"I have it! There is no letter J in the alphabet of these people, so they were forced to use Tch. The inscription means, 'Crown Warrior Jan, Son of the Sun.' This arrow belonged to your boy."

"Crown Warrior," mused Trevor. "What could that be?"

"It says here," continued the don "that it is a title bestowed for distinguished service to the crown. I am of the opinion that your son has found the lost colony of Mu, for which Sir Henry Westgate was searching. And having reached it, he has distinguished himself in some way, earning the title of Crown Warrior. How he attained the hereditary title of 'Sa Re,' I cannot imagine."

"The Indians hereabout all have traditions of an ancient warlike white race living in the interior," said Padre Luis.

"I have listened to these tales many times, but I never believed them."

"If this is Jan's arrow, it follows that he shot the doctor," said Trevor. "I wonder why."

"I believe I can explain that," the *padre* said. "After I had dressed his wound and administered a stimulant, the doctor talked a little. He said he and his men had caught a glimpse of the youth and had followed him, hopping to capture him and bring him in. Jan had suddenly turned and shot him. Bracken apparently did not know that the *señorita* was with Jan that she had been abducted, or that Captain Santos had been slain. I told him he must not do any more talking on account of his injured lung, but he insisted on telling me that much. No doubt he will be able to explain everything shortly."

"In the meantime," said Trevor, "how are we to find Jan?"

"It is my opinion," replied the don, "that in order to find him we must locate this lost colony of Mu. No doubt he is well on his way to his adopted people by this time."

"I'll find it," said Trevor, "if I have to go over the entire South American continent with a fine-toothed comb."

AS JAN, naked and unarmed, sprinted toward the temple ruins with the mob of hairy men in swift pursuit, he suddenly thought of the blowgun and darts he had left in an anteroom some time before. If they were still there and he could but get to that room in time he would give these wild men a surprise.

He dashed through the portal amid a shower of sticks and stones and made straight for his cache.

On reaching it, he found, to his delight, that the weapon and missiles were still there.

Quickly catching the blowgun and the quiver of darts, he loaded the tube and stood in the hallway, waiting. But to his surprise, not one of the hairy men came near. He stood there for some time, and though he could hear the shouts of the wild men outside the temple, he saw no one.

Presently he decided to take a look. He made his way to the portal of the building, cautiously watching for an ambush.

At the portal, he paused. Standing about fifty feet away was a large group of hairy men, chattering excitedly. They seemed afraid to come any nearer. Evidently they were fearful of some danger, fancied or real, in the temple ruins. Something within the building had evidently frightened them before. Perhaps the saber-toothed tiger which had formerly laired there had slain some of their companions. Jan raised his blowgun to his lips. Then he sped a dart at a big hairy fellow who towered above the others. The wild man fell without a sound, and the others stared at him in awed amazement.

Then one of them spied Jan standing in the entrance. With

a loud cry of rage he pointed the youth out to the others. Jan dodged a shower of miscellaneous missiles and brought down another hairy creature with a tiny dart. The entire pack seemed about to charge him.

Suddenly he heard a familiar sound over at his right—the clatter of armored riders and the thunderous tread of their mounts. The hairy men heard it, too, and turning, scampered for the river. But few of them reached it for a troop of the Golden Ones came charging around the side of the ruins with lances couched, pursuing them relentlessly, spitting them on their shafts and riding them down beneath the thundering hoofs.

In the midst of the party rode Mena, Emperor of Satmu, resplendent in his glittering, richly jeweled armor. He caught sight of Jan standing in the portal, and dismounting, walked toward him.

"By the long hairy nose of Anpu!" he said, coming up. "How is it that we find you going about in the costume of a new-born infant? Where are your armor and weapons, and what is that odd-looking tube you carry?"

"My armor and weapons are at the bottom of the river, majesty," replied Jan. "I put them on a raft and went for a swim, but the hairy ones came and overturned them, chasing me into the temple where I found this weapon." He explained the use of the blowgun to the Emperor, and pointed out the bodies of the hairy men who had been slain by the darts.

"A curious and terrible weapon," said Mena. "I'm glad they are not used in Satmu. Leave it here, and come with me. Luckily, the mastodons carry some extra armor, arms and clothing of mine, so we can fit you out again. We'll dress you like an emperor for your triumphal return. You had me worried, Jan. Thought we would never find you. But today we came across the gnawed skeleton of the big sloth you killed, with your broken lance still wedged between its ribs, so I imagined that if you were alive" you would be somewhere hereabout."

"Permit me to thank your majesty for coming to my rescue," said Jan.

"It's all right lad. You came to mine once, didn't you?"

A big mastodon lumbered over at a sign from the monarch.

"Ho, slave!" he called to the driver perched on the woolly neck. "Make the beast kneel. We would get some wearables from that pack."

It was not long before Jan, fully armed and armored once more, was riding beside the Emperor on one of the three-horned mounts. The cavalcade entered Satmu shortly after dark that night.

Jan's return to Satmu was a signal for much rejoicing among its inhabitants, for he had the double distinction of being the Emperor's favorite, and the popular idol as well. Mena held a great feast in honor of the event, which lasted far into the night.

Jan said nothing to any one of his adventures in the jungle. His secret sorrow at Ramona's refusal to return with him was well concealed. Instead of moping about, he worked harder and played harder than ever before. By keeping busy he succeeded in covering up the longing that tugged at his heart.

But try as he would, he could not forget Ramona. He lived over and over again those hours spent in the patio, learning to speak, to write and to draw; and that one outstanding moment in his life when, with arms around his neck and warm lips close to his, she had begged him to take her away with him—to never leave her again.

Then he would wake to stern reality, and go about the business of trying to reshape his life.

CHAPTER XXX

ENEMIES

THUS THE MONTHS passed. A new note of sadness was added when Chicma died of old age and rich living. Having been the pet of the Empress, she was given a royal funeral, and her mummy was laid away in a magnificent sarcophagus in one of the pyramidal mausoleums of the burial grounds of Re.

Like all popular idols Jan had his enemies. Chief among these were Samsu, High Priest of Set, and his craven son, Telapu, whom Jan had ousted. It was popularly conceded that the Emperor would name Jan his heir; but Samsu had other plans.

The black priest, however, was very crafty. Openly, he voiced only admiration for the Emperor's favorite. But several attempts were made on Jan's life. Assassins attacked him by night. Heavy stones mysteriously fell near him from house tops. Once he was near death from poison.

Although Samsu was suspected, there was never the slightest evidence of his guilt. But like all who plot in secret, he finally made a slip that exposed him.

Jan entered his room late one night, tired after a day's hunting. A slave was there to take off his armor, and another to prepare his bath. The room was fully lighted, and everything was apparently as it should be. Yet Jan had a feeling of uneasiness which he could not shake off. Something was wrong. A sixth sense seemed warning him that danger threatened.

Having bathed and donned his silken sleeping garments, he

got into bed. One slave had taken his armor out to be polished. The other snuffed the fragrant oil lamps and departed, leaving him in darkness and silence.

Then Jan realized what had warned him of danger. Above the powerful aroma of the burning lamps, his jungle-trained nostrils had caught the scent of some one—a stranger—there in his room.

For some time Jan lay still, listening tensely. There was no unusual sound. He realized that whoever was in the room would know, by the way he was breathing, that he was not asleep, so he simulated the regular respiration of slumber.

A few minutes later he heard some one slip from behind a tall chest that stood in one corner and stealthily move toward him in the darkness.

Continuing his regular breathing, Jan reached for the heavy stone water bottle that stood on a taboret beside his bed. Then, springing out of bed he hurled it straight at the shadowy form of the marauder. A thud, a gasp, and the sound of a heavy body falling to the floor, told him his missile had struck the mark. He leaped to the door, flinging it wide and admitting the yellow light from the flickering hall lamps.

A black-robed, shaved-headed figure lay upon the floor, moaning and choking. It was the priest Kebshu, first assistant to Samsu. Jan had seen him at court many times with the High Priest of Set. Near his hand lay a long, keen dagger, which he had dropped as he fell.

SOME ONE came along the hallway, stopped in front of the door. Jan looked up. It was Sir Henry Westgate, his arms filled with dusty scrolls from the library. He dropped them, and taking a lamp from its bracket, brought it into the room.

"What's wrong?" he asked. "What has happened?"

"Just another assassin of the Black One," said Jan, wearily. "I hit him with a water bottle and he doesn't seem to recover well."

Sir Henry opened the black robe of the fallen man, revealing a bloody bruise over the heart from which a fractured rib protruded.

"I am dying!" moaned the man on the floor. "There is something—must confess—to Emperor!"

A sentry came clanking along the hallway, stopped, and entered the room.

"Go and ask the Emperor to come here at once," Jan told him.

The guard hurried away.

"Why did you try to kill me?" Jan asked the gasping man on the floor.

"Samsu—made me," was the reply. "Must obey—chief."

Sir Henry shook his head sadly.

Presently Mena arrived, a robe thrown over his sleeping garments. He bent over the recumbent priest.

"Well, Kebshu, you finally got caught in the act," he said, "and having the man, we can easily take the master."

"Must—tell—something, majesty," said Kebshu. "Bend lower—will not be here much longer."

"Go on. I'm listening," said Mena, stooping still lower.

"About your majesty's infant daughter. It was I who stole her, for Samsu. He did not want—heir—stand between Telapu and—throne."

"Villain! What did you do with her?"

"Samsu put her in—floating basket, with—prayer to Hepr. I think that she—that she—" His weak voice trailed into silence. A shudder ran through his frame. Kebshu was dead.

Mena stood up, solemnly raised his right hand, and said:

"By the life of my head and the tombs of my forefathers, I swear that Samsu shall be chained naked on the Rock of Judgment for three days without food or water, that the great god Re may do with him as his wisdom dictates."

Then he turned, and with bowed head, started to walk out of the room. But Sir Henry, who had been listening attentively, suddenly called:

"Majesty!"

The Emperor turned slowly.

"What would your majesty say if I were to tell you that your daughter is probably alive?"

Mena dropped his dejected air, fiercely gripped the wrist of the Englishman.

"What do you mean?"

Westgate told how Don Fernando had found Ramona in a basket.

"You must take me to her!" said Mena. "I will violate every tradition of my ancestors. I will wreck the barriers that shut us off from the outer world which we have not passed for thousands of years, if I can only find my little daughter!"

"That will not be necessary," said Jan of the Jungle. "I can find Ramona for you."

He opened his right hand, displaying the tattooed sacred lotus.

"This was copied from the palm of her right hand," he said. "She taught me to speak, to write, to draw. I begged her to come here with me, but she refused. I was hurt. For that reason I have never gone back."

"But you will go back now," said Mena.

"The Emperor's word is my law," replied Jan. "I leave at dawn."

HARRY TREVOR had left no stone unturned in his search for his lost son. Large parties of his men traversed the jungle from east to west and from north to south, looking for Jan and inquiring about the lost colony of Mu.

When, he saw that his quest might take months, or even years, Trevor brought a large tract of land across the river from the property of Don Fernando. Plans were begun for a palatial home. At the river front he prepared to install concrete docks and a large boathouse for launches, speedboats and canoes. He would also set out thousands of rubber trees, the nucleus of a plantation.

Dr. Bracken's lung recovered, and he again took charge of the jungle sector south of the Suarez plantation. The two Indians who were implicated with Santos in the kidnaping of Ramona had run away. But he kept the others at his base camp, and posted new guards at the tree hut.

Shortly after his arrival there, Dr. Bracken was seated in his cabin one day when a familiar figure appeared in the doorway. With a start, he recognized Santos. The captain's appearance was much changed by a livid scar in the center of his forehead.

"You don' expect to see me again, eh?" said Santos, with a grin.

"One doesn't look for dead men to come to life," replied the doctor, "and you are officially dead. Sit down."

The captain seated himself on a folding stool and lighted a cigarette.

"Was only knock' out for leetle while," he said. "My two Indian come back for gat my gun. They find me sitteeng up. I 'ad stock the 'ut weeth provision, so we stay there. But now I need some theengs. You are my frand. I come to you."

"You made a damn' fool move, kidnaping that girl when you did. But we'll forget that. I can use you if you want to take a little trip for me. I'll put you on a salary and pay all expenses. But of course you'll have to keep under cover."

"I do that, all right. What ees this trip?"

"I want you to go to Caracas for me, to get some things. I'm going to set a trap for Jan that he won't escape. The Indians fired their hypo bullets, all right, but Jan was evidently wearing gold-plated armor. Now this time I'll fix him. Here's what I want."

Closing the door so the Indians would not overhear, he hitched his chair close to that of the captain and gave him his instructions.

That night Santos left for Caracas.

CHAPTER XXXI

DR. BRACKEN'S REVENGE

SOME TWO MONTHS later the captain returned with twenty carriers, all heavily laden. All were paid and dismissed except the two Indians who had previously accompanied him.

During the following week, a circular trench about four feet wide and eight feet deep was dug around the tree which held Jan's hut. A few inches of the top soil and sod were retained, but all other soil taken out was dumped into the stream.

Then many copper wires were stretched about in the trench, after which it was covered with crossed sticks barely strong enough to sustain the earth and sod laid on them. Running from this trench to the doctor's cabin, slightly below the surface of the soil, was a concealed insulated electric cable.

His trap completed, the doctor settled down to await the arrival of his victim. His Indians supposed the trench to be an animal trap. Every time a tapir blundered into it, Bracken pretended to be highly elated, made the necessary repairs, and covered the surface as before.

One night the doctor returned to his cabin, tired out after a long march. He had been to the hacienda on the occasion of Ramona's home-coming from school.

The doctor climbed into his bunk and was just closing his eyes in slumber when the alarm bell sounded on the wall near him. He got up, struck a light, and shut off the alarm. By this time several of his Indians had responded.

"I suppose another confounded tapir has fallen into the pit," he grumbled, as he got into his clothing. "But we'll see."

Carrying flash lights, he and the Indians left for the trap. Walking in the lead, the doctor quickly saw a hole in the thin covering between the tree and the river.

The air was heavy with mingled odors of gas and ether.

The doctor stepped up to the hole, and flashed his light within. Then he gasped in astonishment. His trap contained a victim!

Two Indians came up with stout looped ropes. When they saw what lay in the bottom of the pit, they too gaped in amazement. For it was the body of a man clad from head to foot in shining golden armor.

ONE LOOP was dropped around a foot, and pushed into place with a long pole. The other was dropped around the helmeted head. In a few moments the armored body lay on the surface of the ground.

With his long pole, the doctor shut off the machinery that was flooding the interior of the trench with ether-spray and gas. Then he raised one of his victim's eyelids to note the degree of anaesthesia.

Under his directions, a crude litter was constructed, and in this the insensible one was conveyed to his cabin. The Indians were told to go to their bunks.

As soon as they were gone, the doctor stripped Jan of his armor and clothing. Then he fashioned a crude garment for him from one of his jaguar skins, and dragged him into the cage. From his medicine case, he took a bottle marked with the Latin name, "Cannabis indica."

When Jan showed signs of returning consciousness, Bracken prepared a solution of the hashish, which he gave him to drink. Then the victim relapsed into a drugged slumber, and the doctor went back to his bunk.

For more than two weeks the doctor kept Jan under the influence of hashish, that drug which changes the gentlest of men to dangerous, insane killers. Hashish, the mind-destroyer, from which we have derived our word "assassin."

It was his purpose to undermine Jan's mentality by drugs and hypnotic suggestion, until Jan had reverted to the stage at which he escaped from the menagerie and would be therefore subject to the doctor's control as he had been during his life behind the bars of a cage.

Dr. Bracken also constructed a cage on wheels, a narrow affair that could be dragged along the jungle paths cleared by *machetes*. When all was ready, he traveled north until he came within striking range of his victim, Georgia Trevor. An Indian was dispatched to circle the plantation and come back from the north with the report that Jan had been seen in that direction.

From his place of concealment, the doctor grinned his triumph as he saw Harry Trevor and Don Fernando leave with a party of searchers, following their false informant.

He waited for darkness, then saw to it that his stage was properly set. Georgia Trevor, he observed, was alone in the living room of the cottage they were occupying while the big house was being built.

After leaving instructions with Santos and the two Indians who waited in the shadows with the caged Jan, he walked boldly up to the front door and entered.

Georgia Trevor, who had been reading, started up in astonishment at his abrupt entrance.

"You!" she said. "I thought it was Harry, coming back."

"I have a surprise for you," he announced. "Remain where you are."

"You don't mean—?"

"But I do. I've found your son. I've found Jan."

There was the sound of shuffling feet—something sliding across the porch toward the door.

The doctor clapped his hands. A figure shambled into the

room, walking ape-like on toes and knuckles—a redheaded youth whose sole garment was a tattered jaguar skin.

Georgia Trevor gazed at the figure, horrified, fascinated, as a bird gazes at a serpent about to devour it. Jan's eyes stared wildly back at her—devoid of reason, menacing.

"Madame," said the doctor, "behold your son." Then he suddenly clapped his hands, and cried:

"Mother! Kill!"

He watched gloatingly as with a horrible bestial roar, the drug-crazed Jan charged straight for the woman who had borne him.

RAMONA SUAREZ drew the prow of her canoe up on the dock in front of the Trevor cottage. The doña had gone to bed with a headache, leaving Ramona to her own devices, and the girl had decided that she would cross the river and spend the evening with Georgia Trevor.

As she walked up the sloping lawn toward the house, she noticed a shadowy something on the front porch.

There seemed to be a cart at the bottom of the steps, and from this two men were sliding a tall, narrow cage toward the door. She walked closer, then gave a little gasp of surprise for by the lamplight that streamed out from the house she saw that Jan was in the cage. It was being moved by Santos and one of the Indians who had abducted her. Although she had no inkling of the purpose behind these actions, she knew that it could not be other than evil. She must warn Jan's mother.

Keeping in the shadow of the shrubbery, she ran lightly around to the side of the house. A French window stood open, and there was a screen door on that side of the porch. She tried the door, found it unlocked, and stepped silently inside. Through the French window she saw Georgia Trevor, pale and frightened, standing beside her chair. Advancing toward her with a peculiar, ape-like walk and the look of an insane killer in his bloodshot eyes, was Jan.

She heard the words of the doctor: "Madame, behold your son," and his command, "Mother! Kill!"

As Jan emitted his terrible roar and charged, Ramona ran between him and his mother.

"Jan! Jan!" she cried. "What are you doing? Stop!"

Jan paused, stood erect, staring fixedly at her as if trying to evoke some lost memory.

The doctor seized her by the arm, jerked her roughly aside.

"Keep out of this, you little foot!" he snarled.

Some thought, some suggestion penetrated Jan's hypnotized, drug-fogged mind as the doctor dragged the girl aside. This girl was his. Some one—it must be an enemy—was hurting her.

With a second roar as thunderous as the first, he charged again, but this time at the doctor.

Ramona covered her eyes with her hands. There were groans, snarls, thuds curses—the snapping of human bones and the rending of human flesh. Then an ominous stillness, broken only by some one's loud, labored breathing.

Suddenly Ramona was caught up as lightly as if she had been a child and carried out of the house, across the lawn, through the rows of young rubber trees, into the darkness of the jungle.

WEEKS LATER, Harry Trevor and his wife were following four Indians who carried in a litter, a hideous, misshapen wreck of a man. One eyelid sagged in an empty socket.

An ear was missing. Where the nose should have been, a small square of surgical gauze was held in place by bits of crossed tape. The arms and legs were twisted and useless.

When it was found that the mangled form of Dr. Bracken had some life in it an Indian had been dispatched for Padre Luis. But he had returned with the news that the good *padre* had gone on a mission in the interior, and would be gone for weeks. It was a journey of two weeks to the nearest surgeon, and it would take him two more weeks to return. By that time it would be too late to set the doctor's broken arms and legs. And he was so near death that he could not travel.

So the woman and man he had devoted the best years of his life to injuring, nursed him and did the best they could to maintain his flickering spark of life.

He had recovered sufficiently in six weeks to stand travel in a litter, and Harry Trevor was sending him to Bolivar for surgical attention.

As the Indians carefully deposited the litter in the boat, a canoe drew up beside it and grounded against the sloping landing. A tall straight clean-limbed young man with the features of a Greek god crowned by a tumbling mass of auburn curls sprang lightly out. He stood for a moment, smiling at the couple who stood on the dock staring at him as if they could not believe their eyes.

His silken garments, decked with gold and jewels worth a fortune, were those of another age. Jewels blazed from the golden hilts of the sword and dagger that hung from his belt.

"Father! Mother!" he said, holding out his arms. "I am your son, Jan. I have come back to you because—because we need each other."

The hideous wreck in the litter cocked its good eye up at the little group on the dock—saw Jan embrace his father, kiss his mother, whose auburn head barely reached to his shoulder. With a shudder Dr. Bracken turned away from the sight of his ruined plan for revenge.

"Where is Ramona?" Jan's mother asked.

"She is with her father and mother," replied Jan. "Her real father and mother. She's a royal princess, you know. I just came from the hacienda. Carried a message to the don and doña for her. She will live with her own parents, but has promised to visit them often."

"And you, Jan—my son! My boy! You will stay with us, won't you, now that we've found you after all these years? Think of it! I have always thought of you as a baby, for all those years, but I find you grown up—a man."

"Of course I'll stay, mother, for a while. And I'll come back often. But next month you must come with me for a visit. Preparations are being made for a royal wedding, and I wouldn't want to keep Ramona waiting."

"Jan! You mean that you two are going to be married?"

"Of course. And mother, other than you, she is the most wonderful girl in all the world."

ABOUT THE AUTHOR

WRITING, WITH ME, is a semi-subjective process. I mean by this that I find it necessary, at times, to wait for that temperamental and elusive entity, my Muse, to cooperate with me. Every day I try to write, and I mean *try*. But some days I produce only a few hundred words fit for nothing but filing in the wastebasket. And on the other hand I have, in a single day, produced six or seven thousand words of marketable copy.

So this, the problem of successfully wooing the Muse, is the one which I find most difficult of solution. I have a profound admiration for writers who can sit down at their desks, day after day, and, without fail, bat out two or three thousand words of good, salable material in two or three hours. Most of them will tell you this is the result of practice of continuous trying. But I've been trying for ten years, and selling stories for eight, and today my Muse is as obstinate and capricious as ever.

Although I had previously written songs, plays, and moving picture scenarios, my first inspiration for writing fiction, strange as it may seem, came from reading books on psychology. And that reading was the result of some previous incidents in my life, so perhaps I had better begin a little farther back.

When I graduated from high school, I decided that I would launch on a musical career, and gave up my plans for going to college. I became a professional songwriter. I also tried my hand at plays and moving picture scenarios, and wrote vaudeville sketches and even plots for burlesque shows. I later became a music publisher. But it was a hard life, with much night work, plugging songs in theatres, dance halls, and cafes, and I tired of it, in spite of the fascination the element of chance gave to the work.

Putting out songs was like playing poker; no one could predict a hit with certainty.

I decided on a business career, and went to a business college. Shortly after this, I got a job, and at twenty-

Otis Adelbert Kline

two I married. No chance, then, to go to college. But going to college had been a sort of tradition in our family. I had to work every day to keep the well-known and justly unpopular wolf from breaking down the door. But my evenings were my own. I decided to use them for the improvement of what I optimistically called my mind.

I would take one subject at a time, and study. But where should I begin? I recalled that a certain ancient philosopher had once said there are but three things in the universe—mind, force, and matter. Mind controls force, and force moves matter. It was easy to decide which of these things was the more important, so I began by studying psychology—a science which, by the way, is in its infancy—no farther advanced today than were the physical sciences a century ago.

Having read practically everything there was on the subject over a period of years, I began to have some theories about psychic phenomena, myself. I started a ponderous scientific treatise, but didn't carry it far. This medium limited my imagination too much. Then I wrote a novelette, "The Thing of a Thousand Shapes," in which some of my ideas and theories were incorporated. It was turned down by most of the leading magazines in 1922, but early in 1923 a magazine was made to order for the story—*Weird Tales*. It was accepted, and published in the first issue. This was before the word "ectoplasm" was used in connection with psychic phenomena. A German writer, whose translated work I had read, had coined the word "tele-plasm," but this did not seem precisely the right term, so I coined the word "psychoplasm." I notice that it is being used today by some writers of occult stories.

I had finished writing the above novelette early in 1921, and decided to try my hand at a novel. I wanted to write an inter-planetary story, and I believe the reason for this lay in the fol-lowing incidents.

As soon as I was able to understand, my father, who was interested in all the sciences, and especially in astronomy, had begun pointing out to me the planets that were visible to the naked eye; had told me what was known of their masses, den-sities, surfaces, atmospheres, motions, and satellites; and that there was a possibility that some of them were inhabited by living beings. He taught me how to find the Big and Little Dippers, and thus locate the North Star, that I might make the heavens serve as a compass for me, by night as well as by day. He pointed out that beautiful and mysterious constellation, The Pleiades, which inspired the lines in the Book of Job: "Canst thou bind the sweet influences of Pleiades, or loose the bonds of Orion?"

He told me of the vast distances which, according to the computations of scientists, lay between our world and these twinkling celestial bodies—that the stars were suns, some smaller than our own, and others so large that if they were hollow, our entire Solar System could operate inside them without danger of the planet farthest from the sun striking the shell. He told me of the nebulae, which might be giant uni-verses in the making, and that beyond the known limits of our own universe it was possible that there were countless others, stretching on into infinity.

My childish imagination had been fired by these things, and I had read voraciously such books on the subject of astronomy as were available in my father's well-stocked library. He supple-mented and encouraged this reading by many interesting discussions, in which a favorite subject for speculation was the possibility that planets, other than our own, were inhabited.

Geology, archaeology, and ethnology were also brought into our discussions. We lived in northern Illinois, which had in some distant geological epoch been the bottom of an ocean, and took pleasure in collecting such fossil remains as were available. Dad and I could become very much excited over bits of coral, and fossil marine animals.

Then there were Darwin, Huxley, Tyndall, and others, with their interesting theories. There was the great mystery of man's advent on this earth, which religion explained in one manner and science in another. We discussed these, and a third possibility, an idea of my father's, that some of our ancient civilizations might have been originated by people who came here from other planets—the science of space-navigation forgotten by their descendants, but the tradition of their celestial advent persisting in their written and oral traditions. That such traditions did persist was beyond dispute. Whence came these traditions that were not confined to related civilizations, but were preserved by widely separated peoples?

It was with this background that I began my first novel in 1921—a tale of adventures on the planet Venus. I called it *Grandon of Terra*, but the name was later changed to *The Planet of Peril*.

The problem of how to get my hero to Venus bothered me not at all, for I had been reading about the marvelous powers of the subjective mind: of telepathy, that mysterious means of communication between minds which needs no physical media for its transmission, and which seems independent of time, space, and matter. I haven't the space to enlarge on this here, but can refer you to the thousands of cases recorded by the British Society for Psychical Research, if you are interested. There was also the many cases of so-called astral projection, recorded by the above society in a volume called Phantasms of the Living. My hero, therefore, reached Venus by the simple (try it) expedient of exchanging bodies with a young man on that planet who was his physical twin. He reported his adventures on Venus to an earthly scientist, Dr. Morgan, by telepathy.

Cloud-wrapped Venus is supposed to be in a stage similar to our own carboniferous era. I, therefore, clothed my hypothetical Venus with the flora of such an era-ferns, cycads, and thallophytes of many kinds, including algae, fungi, and lichens of strange and eerie form.

Through the fern jungles and fungoid forests stalked gigantic reptiles, imaginary creatures, but analogous to those ponderous prehistoric Saurians that roved the earth when our coal and petroleum beds were having their inception. There were Herbivora devouring the primitive plants, and fierce Carnivora that devoured the Herbivora and each other, and disputed the supremacy of man. Air and water teemed with active life and sudden dealt-life feeding on death and death snuffing out life.

There were men in various stages of evolutionary development—men without eyes, living in lightless caverns, who had degenerated to a physical and mental condition little better than that of Batrachia. There were monkey-men swinging through the branches and lianas of the fern forests, blood-sucking bat-men living in caves in a volcanic crater—a veritable planetary inferno, and gigantic termites of tremendous mental development that had enslaved a race of primitive human beings.

There were mighty empires, whose armies warred with strange and terrible weapons, and airships which flew at tremendous speed propelled by mechanisms which amplified the power of mind over matter—telekinesis.

After writing and rewriting, polishing and re-polishing, I sent the story out—a bulky script, ninety-thousand words long. At that time there but two possible American markets for that type of story, *Science and Invention* and *Argosy-All Story*, but I had not been watching the Munsey publication and did not know it used this sort of tiling. I submitted the story, first, to

Science and Invention. It was turned down because of the paucity of mechanical science.

When *Weird Tales* came into being, I tried it on this magazine. Edwin Baird, the editor liked it, but finally, after holding it several months, rejected it because of its length. He suggested that I try *Argosy-All Story*, but I didn't do it then. I let it lie around for a long time. Every once in a while I would dig it out of the file and read it over. Each time, I found new places to polish. I was writing and selling a number of other stories in the interval-occult, weird, mystery, detective, adventure, and Western. I also collaborated with my brother, Allen S. Kline, on a novel set in the South American jungle, called *The Secret Kingdom*. This was later published in *Amazing Stories*.

One day I was talking to Baird, and he asked me what I had done with my fantastic novel. He said I was foolish not to try *Argosy-All Story*. I accordingly recopied my pencil-marked version, and sent it on. Good old Bob Davis, dean of American editors, held it so long I had some hope: that he was going to buy it. But it came back, eventually, with a long, friendly letter asking to see more of my work. I later learned that he had just bought the first of Ralph Milne Farley's famous Radio stories, the scene of which was on the planet Venus, and whose settings, therefore, were somewhat similar to mine.

After that, I spent enough money on express and postage to buy a good overcoat, sending the story around the country, and out of it.

Finally, Mr. Joseph Bray then book-buyer, and now president of A.C. McClurg & Company, told me he would publish it if I would first get it serialized in a magazine. I had turned down a couple of low-priced offers for serialization, but I started over the list again. A.H. Bittner, the new editor of *Argosy*, who has been building circulation for that magazine since he took over the editorial chair, bought the story. A month later, Mr. Bray accepted it for publication as a novel.

The Planet of Peril brought many enthusiastic fan letters to

Argosy. I received a number of complimentary letters from people all over the country who had read it in magazine or book form. I was overwhelmed with requests for autographs, and all that sort of thing. A baby in Battle Creek, Michigan, was named after me. It was encouraging.

Last September, Grosset & Dunlap reprinted the book in the popular edition. In a bulletin to their salesmen they recently reported that, despite the fact that they had not made any special effort to push it, and that it was a first novel, it was enjoying a continuous and persistent resale—something unusual for a first novel. They suggested that their salesmen remember this item when calling on the trade. This, also, was encouraging.

Since then, *Argosy* has serialized and McClurg has published in book form two more novels—*Maza of the Moon* and *The Prince of Peril,* the latter a companion story to *The Planet of Peril.*

Right now I'm working night and day on a new novel for spring publication, in order to make a deadline date set by my publisher.

TARZAN
AND THE JEWELS
OF OPAR
BY ARGOSY'S GREATEST AUTHOR
EDGAR RICE BURROUGHS®

WAR LORD
OF MANY
SWORDSMEN
W. WIRT

CLOVELLY
BY WORLD-FAMOUS AUTHOR
MAX BRAND

DRINK
WE DEEP
THE SCIENCE FICTION CLASSIC
ARTHUR LEO ZAGAT

THE GUN-
BRAND
BY NORTHWEST FICTION LEGEND
JAMES B. HENDRYX

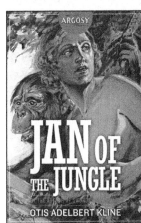

JAN OF
THE JUNGLE
OTIS ADELBERT KLINE

THE BLUE
FIRE PEARL
GEORGE F. WORTS

THE MOON
POOL
& THE CONQUEST OF
THE MOON POOL
ABRAHAM MERRITT

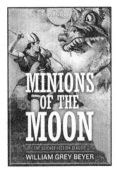

MINIONS
OF THE
MOON
THE SCIENCE FICTION CLASSIC
WILLIAM GREY BEYER

ALIAS THE
NIGHT WIND
VARICK VANARDY

THE ARGOSY LIBRARY ™

SERIES 3 INCLUDES:

* BURROUGHS * ZAGAT * MERRITT *
* BRAND * KLINE *
* BEYER * HENDRYX *
* WIRT * VANARDY *
* WORTS *

THE BEST FICTION
FROM THE FRANK
A. MUNSEY LINE

Made in the USA
Coppell, TX
12 July 2021